SNOW APPLES

Snow Apples

MARY RAZZELL

Groundwood Books

HOUSE OF ANANSI PRESS
TORONTO   BERKELEY

Groundwood Books / House of Anansi Press
110 Spadina Avenue, Suite 801, Toronto, Ontario M5V 2K4
Distributed in the USA by Publishers Group West
1700 Fourth Street, Berkeley, CA 94710

We acknowledge for their financial support of our publishing program the
Canada Council for the Arts, the Government of Canada through the Book
Publishing Industry Development Program (BPIDP) and the
Ontario Arts Council.

ONTARIO ARTS COUNCIL
CONSEIL DES ARTS DE L'ONTARIO

Library and Archives Canada Cataloguing in Publication
Razzell, Mary
Snow apples / Mary Razzell.
First published: Vancouver: Groundwood Books / Douglas & McIntyre, 1984
ISBN-13: 978-0-88899-741-8 (bound) ISBN-10: 0-88899-741-8 (bound)
ISBN-13: 978-0-88899-728-9 (pbk.) ISBN-10: 0-88899-728-0 (pbk.)
I. Title.
PS8585.A99S66 2006   jC813'.54   C2005-906986-4

Design by Michael Solomon
Cover photograph by Tim Fuller
Printed and bound in Canada

With thanks to the late Carol Shields,
who encouraged me to tell what it was really like
to be a young girl at that time.

1

"DOES SHE scare you?" I asked Sonia. We had just jumped down from the school bus after classes, and we could see Helga Ness come out of the woods on one side of the road and start down the beach trail on the other. She looked skinny and old, and her running shoes flopped. Her eyes darted nervously at us, then away. Her dress was faded, with only traces of the original pattern remaining.

"A little..." said Sonia. "Look at her. Why is she always carrying a stick and hitting the salal bushes?"

"I don't know," I answered. "It's like she's angry or something."

"Maybe she's crazy."

I agreed. "And she's always talking to herself."

Helga was an old Norwegian woman who lived near us, and I often passed her on the way to the store.

"Are you coming to my place today, Sheila?" Sonia asked.

"Oh, I wish I could." It was true. I'd rather go to Sonia Kolosky's house than my own. I felt more at home there, if only because her mother treated me as if I was a nice person. My mother had a way of making me feel the exact opposite. "But I have to pick up the mail and go right home. My mother says I spend too much time at your house."

Before Sonia's family moved to the Landing from Saskatchewan a year earlier, I was so lonely, I thought I would die. We'd moved here ourselves from Edmonton two years before, and there were no other families with children. When the Koloskys came with their five boys and five girls—and all looking like Mrs. Kolosky, with blonde hair and pale blue eyes—the census was raised to forty-three. There must have been a Mr. Kolosky because there was a small baby, but no one had ever seen him.

There were other girls at the school at Gibson's Landing, four miles away, but almost all of us went in by bus or boat, so there were no after-school friendships for me. Until Sonia.

If I'd met Sonia in Edmonton I doubt that we would have become friends. For one thing, she was only fourteen, and I was almost sixteen. And we were too different. I would have been too busy going to the library or Guides with friends I'd known since grade school. Sonia was more a home person. She was like a second mother in that house on the Upper Road.

I loved being in that house. Mrs. Kolosky was as plain and wholesome as a parsnip, but she treated me like I was kid number eleven in her brood.

I was thinking all these things as I waved goodbye to Sonia and headed down the road to the village store and post office.

Then, all of a sudden, the world seemed to split apart with noise.

There was a series of loud blasts from fish boats out in the Sound. I could see a tug circling round and round in a tight circle, and all the time it was blowing its whistle. Seagulls shrieked and scattered. Frightened birds flew in clouds from the trees on the side of the road.

I ran toward the beach. There was Helga Ness trying to drag her old boat from above the tide level down to the water's edge. She was pushing and shoving and straining like a crazy woman.

I felt I had to go over to help her. Together we got it into the ocean. She hesitated a moment, then looked at me as if she wanted me to get in. I didn't want to, but that's what she seemed to want, so I pushed the boat out and we both hopped in. Helga started the motor, and we headed out to the nearest fish boat to see what the trouble was.

As soon as we got close enough to the *Nancy D*, she called out to the skipper, "Did you find them?"

"I don't know who you mean, missus," he shouted back. "All I know is that it's VE Day. The war is over. The war is over, thank God!" And he pulled on the boat's whistle once again.

Helga's head sank onto her bony chest, and she slumped as if she'd been hit. I had to reach around her to grab the rudder to straighten out the boat.

By the time I got the boat back to shore, Helga was sitting up again, staring out at the sea. I pulled the boat up as far as I could and tied it to one of the logs that lay above the line of dried seaweed ribboning the shore. But by the time I had finished, Helga was already off the sand and heading up the pine-needled beach trail.

Before she turned off the trail, she looked around and saw me watching her. The look in her eyes made me flinch, it was so desolate.

* * *

"There you are, Sheila. Two letters for your mother today." Mr. Percy slid them through the wicket.

Mr. Percy runs the village store and post office, and there is nothing in the village that he doesn't know about. Some people say that he isn't above holding the mail up to the light, but I think it has to do with his eyebrows. They are thick and peaked, and when Mr. Percy gets interested in anything, his eyebrows rise higher and higher until they almost disappear into his hair. I've found myself telling

Mr. Percy's eyebrows things that I would never tell anyone else.

"Did you hear the good news?" he said. "The war is over. It's VE Day, Victory Day in Europe. It's just come over the radio."

I told him about Helga. "What did she mean, Mr. Percy? 'Did you find them?' Find who?"

Mr. Percy sighed. "Her two boys and her husband. They drowned in a canoeing accident. The bodies were never found. It was before you folks moved here."

The old wooden clock over the counter ticked away our thoughts. Mr. Percy busied himself at the ice box. He handed me an opened bottle of 7-Up, then popped another one for himself.

"This is a day for celebration, nonetheless. A day for the history books. You can tell your children that there you were, fourteen years old…"

"Fifteen, I'm almost sixteen," I interrupted.

"…and stood on the beach and watched the fish boats and tugs celebrate the defeat of Adolf Hitler. It's a day we've all been praying for."

* * *

My mother wasn't pleased that I was late. I could tell by the way she rammed the alder wood into the stove and let the lid go bang. So before I hung up my jacket, I started talking. I told her about Helga, and about the war being over, and by the time I had finished explaining, I had the potatoes out of the cooler.

Out of the corner of my eye, I saw her sit down suddenly at the kitchen table.

"Well, I never," she said. She sat still for a long time, which in itself was unusual because she was always moving, always busy. Even when she sat, her hands were occupied, mending or knitting.

I finished peeling the potatoes, put them in a blackened pot and set the pot on the hottest part of the stove.

Still she sat.

"You want carrots?" I asked.

"Um, yes. You know what this means, don't you? The war over and all…" My lateness was completely forgotten. "It means your father will be back home." She marched her fingernails on the table like so many troops. "And he'll be out of work, as per usual. At least with him in the service, I could be sure a check was coming in every month."

I stiffened. As I cleaned the carrots, I thought about my parents. My mother is fifteen years younger than my father but you'd never know it. She acts older. I wondered why she said she loved him but was always complaining about everything he did. And, if he loved her, why did he cause her worry about money and food and taking care of us kids?

It had been this way as far back as I could remember. It was a relief for her when he joined the air force. He had lied about his age to get in; he was fifty-five but looked forty.

For the first time she had enough money, as she said, "to keep the home together."

I set the table around my mother. She was scribbling something on the back of a used envelope—adding, subtracting, calculating. It seemed to work out all right in the end, because she got up briskly and reached for the frying pan.

The sausages were a crisp brown by the time I heard my brothers outside. Their timing, as usual, was perfect. You could call and search and never find them, but have a meal ready to be put on the table, and they would appear out of nowhere. I considered it a special talent of theirs.

Paul, my oldest brother, was away in the air force. That left three brothers at home. Tom was fourteen, and being so close in age, we were rivals in everything, from who got the highest marks at school to who could stay up latest at night. Jim was eleven and Mike was ten.

They were good-looking boys, even if they were my brothers. Everyone said so. It griped me that they had the best features of both parents or else—somehow—it looked better on them. But my mother just told me, "It's what's inside that's important."

She was strong on character. That was the big difference between my parents. My father thought the here and now were to be enjoyed. She thought we would be rewarded later, when we died and went to heaven. In the meantime there was work to be done and responsibilities to be met. Dad loved to drink beer and talk. She wanted the outhouse whitewashed and some money put aside for a rainy day.

My mother said I took after my father, and the way she said it, this was not a good thing. It was true that we both had brown eyes and dark skin that tanned quickly in the summer, but it was my character, or lack of it, that she meant.

The boys came in with armfuls of wood and cedar kindling. Jim and Mike had been riding horses, they said. This was free-range country, and it wasn't much trouble to get hold of a horse if you wanted one.

Tom smelled of fish and salt water. The cat roused herself from the couch and coiled herself around his legs so that he couldn't move to unload his armful of wood.

"Sheila," he said, "unwind this animal from me." As I moved closer to him, I caught a glimpse of a cigarette package in his jacket pocket. I had one on him now, something that would counter any threat of him telling that I wore lipstick at school.

When we were seated at the table for dinner, I couldn't help smiling at Tom.

"What's the matter with you?" he asked suspiciously.

"Nothing," I answered. We were back to a normal day. Helga, the shrill whistles of the circling fish boats, the German surrender, my father's homecoming—they had all faded to the background. Our hands reached for the food.

"Sheila, Tom, Jim, Mike." My mother strung our names out in a litany. "We will say grace first, please."

"Bless us, O Lord, and these thy gifts…" I sneaked a look at the plate of sausages. There were eighteen. That meant three each and one extra for the boys because my mother said they needed more protein for growing than girls did. "…Amen."

2

SO THAT was Tuesday. VE Day, May 9, 1945. The day Mr. Percy said would go down in the history books.

The girls' basketball team was to play against Port Mellon on the Victoria Day weekend, and I was one of the forwards. Sonia was the other. A fish boat had been hired by the school board to take us up to Port Mellon, a pulp-mill town whose smell often drifted down the Sound, depending on which way the wind blew.

"Do you think there will be any cute guys there?" I asked Sonia as we huddled together at the stern of the *Mimi 1*. The smell of the diesel was rich with adventure, the sound of the engine was music.

Sonia shrugged. She didn't really care.

I did. My mother accused me of being boy-crazy, and

for once I had to agree with her. I felt kind of funny around boys. Too excited. Too interested. At the same time, I was afraid of them because of the longings they caused.

Even in Edmonton when I had been a couple of years younger, I'd felt it. One of the neighbor boys my age had been kicking a soccer ball around, and it had landed in front of me. Without thinking, I'd grabbed it and started running. He had run after me and tackled, and we'd rolled around on the grass. There had been a sharp rapping on the window, and my mother had called me in.

"No more wrestling with boys," she'd said. I'd acted as if I didn't know what she'd meant, but I had been aware of the sharp, sweet ache within me when I had been on the ground with the boy above me, his head blotting out the sun, a halo around his head. I had felt dizzy, scared, stirred.

* * *

We were in the last quarter of the game. The score was tied. The Port Mellon team had a loud cheering section. We had no one because there hadn't been room on the fish boat. To make matters worse, a male voice was making rude remarks every time I got hold of the ball.

"Who is that creep?" I asked one of the Port Mellon girls when a time-out was called for a foul.

"Bob McLean. His father runs the mill." Then there was no more time for conversation because the whistle blew, and the game was on again.

Sonia got the ball and passed it to me. I was at the

halfway line of the court, and I pivoted, looking for Sonia to move forward toward our basket.

"Watch the dum-dum drop it!" Bob McLean yelled from the bleachers.

I pivoted again, and with the momentum of that plus the anger that exploded inside me, I brought the ball up from my side in a great sweeping arc. The ball swished through the net without even touching the rim.

No one was more astonished than I was. Back of the whistling and applauding, I heard Bob McLean again.

"Wow-eee," he called.

At the dance following the game, he came straight over to me. I expected him to be conceited, and he was.

He had every reason to be. He looked like an ad for tennis sweaters: good-looking, well built. I couldn't help wondering why he was bothering with me. He could have had any girl there.

"You're pretty good," he said.

If I'd been honest, I would have told him it had just been a lucky shot. But I just smiled.

"Let's get out of here," he said, "and go over to my house and listen to records. Do you like Jackie Teagarden?"

It didn't occur to me not to go. This was what I'd come to Port Mellon for. But still, I had to be careful.

"I can only stay a little while. I don't want to miss the boat home."

"We'll be back in plenty of time," he promised.

We walked along the wooden sidewalks that led from

the community hall past all the identical houses where the mill workers lived. The windows were curtainless, and I could see the workers in their kitchens, suspenders down, underwear showing. One had a radio on loudly. From another house I heard the wail of a baby.

At our right were the buildings of the mill. Naked light bulbs hung high, showing the heavy wooden beams supporting the structures. The saws whined, and the wood shrieked as if the logs were being desecrated.

The McLean house was far from the sound of the mill and set in the middle of a terraced garden. From the living room we could see the glow of the lights of Vancouver reflected in the southern sky. Out in the night, frogs croaked.

Bob's parents were out for the evening. They never minded, he told me, if he brought someone home even if they weren't there.

He let me choose the records while he got the fireplace going. He had Benny Goodman, Frank Sinatra—everything. When the logs had caught and the flames were dancing flickers up the chimney, Bob went out into the kitchen and made us each a cup of hot chocolate.

While we drank that, I looked around. I'd never been in a house like this before. Leather chairs and books and rich oil paintings of cedar trees and Indian totems and logged-off mountains. Then I felt his arm on my shoulders as he turned me to kiss him. In the background Bunny Berrigan was singing: "I've flown around the world in a plane/I've settled revolutions in Spain/Now the North Pole I have charted/Still I can't get started with you."

I was beginning to come apart inside. Bob touched my breast. But then he got up abruptly and turned away from me, going to the picture window to stare out at the stars.

Had I put him off somehow?

When he came back to stand in front of me, he just said in a serious voice, "Come on. Let's go back now."

The dance was beginning to break up by the time we got back. Bob walked with me down to the government float where the *Mimi 1* was tied up.

"I'll write you," he said, "and I'll come down to see you. How about next weekend? Would that be all right with your family? I could come down Friday night and leave on the Sunday noon boat."

Did he mean stay at my house? I was so astounded, I couldn't answer. He kissed me goodbye in front of everybody.

Even when the lights of Port Mellon had faded in the distance, I was still numb. His was obviously a world I knew nothing about. Maybe his parents didn't mind if he had guests, even overnight ones. My mother would have a fit. I already slept on a cot in the living room. My three brothers slept in one of the two bedrooms, Mom and Dad (when he was home on leave) in the other. We had calendars on the walls, not oil paintings. The dishes didn't match. There was no bathroom, just the outhouse down a little path and shielded by alders.

It was impossible.

"But, oh, Sonia," I said, turning to her there on the *Mimi 1* on our way home through the darkness. "Just think! He wanted to."

* * *

I woke up the next morning at ten. Pep, our dog, was barking and tugging at the sleeve of my nightgown.

"Mom!" But there was no answer. She must have been out working in the barn.

I hurried to dress. What could be the matter? Pep kept whining and running around in a tight circle. Perhaps Jim or Mike was in trouble. This was the day they were going to catch Big Red and try to ride him.

Big Red was one of a band of horses that ran free-range on the peninsula, practically wild. Jim and Mike swore they would catch Big Red one day and ride him.

Pep ran ahead of me, barking and turning every so often to make sure I was following him. He led me along the side of the creek toward the base of the mountain.

Ten minutes in, I saw a piece of Jim's red shirt caught on a blackberry vine. A little farther on there were fresh orange peels curled in a fern. Around me robins sang of summer coming.

Pep was snuffling along the trail, slobbering in his excitement. And then, there was Jim lying across the trail, his head in a pool of blood.

I could see the deep gash over his left ear. The blood was

a dark crimson and oozed slowly. I had to fight panic when I couldn't rouse him. It was as though he were in a deep sleep.

I quickly took off the white blouse and flowered dirndl skirt I wore and then my slip. The slip was an old cotton one but clean, and I thought it would do to make a pad to staunch the flow of blood matting the pine needles on the trail. I wadded it under Jim's head. Using my fingers, I pressed hard on the upper side of the gash until the bleeding stopped. But every time I took my fingers away, the blood would begin to seep again.

I remembered that my mother used to mix saliva and sugar to stop any of our badly bleeding cuts. Jim had some sugar cubes for the horses in his pocket. I put a couple in my mouth. The minute they dissolved, I let the mixture drop into the wound to mix with the blood. It seemed to work.

Pulling on my skirt and buttoning my blouse, I went to look for Mike. Pep stayed with Jim, laying his nose on his paws and watching him, all the time making a high-pitched whine.

I heard Mike moaning. He was about thirty feet away. His freckles stood out against the whiteness of his face. I'd never known he had so many. Or noticed how small he was, lying down. One of his legs was at a crazy angle.

Kneeling beside him, I said, "I'm going for help. Jim's unconscious. What happened?"

He stopped moaning. He looked scared.

"Big Red spooked when we were on him, and we... went flying. Hurry, Sheila."

I ran. I scrambled over fallen trees. Tore through blackberry vines. Thundered over the wooden bridge. Damp. Breathless. Scared. Wondering how I could get help quickly.

There was Helga Ness at work in her vegetable garden, an old gunny sack around her waist for an apron. I hesitated to tell her what had happened. But I was afraid to take the time to find my mother.

She surprised me.

"Get Mr. Percy," she told me. Then she took off for her woodshed and was already putting a chainsaw on a packboard when I left.

When Mr. Percy and I arrived back in his truck, she had everything ready for us. Mr. Percy took the chainsaw. I had two blankets and a coil of rope to carry. She took a machete.

Mr. Percy went ahead and cleared the trail of windfalls. Helga slashed at the blackberry vines, and I came behind clearing away the debris. It seemed to take forever, and all I could think of was the blood oozing out of Jim's head, and Mike's twisted leg.

There at last was Jim, just as I had left him, lying in the same position and still unconscious, a large clot formed on the wound. I ran over to where Mike lay. There was a film of sweat on his forehead. I held his hand, something I'd never done before.

"Mr. Percy and Mrs. Ness are here. He's going to carry you, and Mrs. Ness and I will take Jim. It's going to be all right now, Mike." I felt him squeeze my hand.

Helga and I carefully worked one of the blankets under Jim. It was hard to remember that I had thought of her as crazy when her hands were now so capable.

Mr. Percy tied the corners of the blanket securely to two poles so that we had a makeshift stretcher. With Helga in the lead, she and I carried Jim back down the trail. Mr. Percy put a splint on Mike's leg, wrapped him in a blanket and carried him out of the forest down to Helga's place.

Although we didn't say anything to each other, Helga and I worked well together. She seemed to know when my arms felt as if they were coming out of their sockets. I noticed when her feet dragged on the ground. When that happened, we set Jim down gently on the path and rested.

It was strange to hear the birds still singing and see bright new green ferns unfurled on the forest floor. The air smelled sweet and warm.

When we had rested for a minute, we moved together to pick up the stretcher and walk again.

Mr. Percy arrived just behind us at the Ness yard. We put Jim down in the shade of the woodshed and while Mr. Percy continued to hold Mike, we followed his brief orders to place a mattress on the flatbed of his truck. There we made the boys as secure as possible by tying them down with rope. I knelt between them and hung on by hooking one hand through the open back window of the cab.

A couple of quick turns of the crank and Mr. Percy had the engine running.

"I think we should get your mother before we head for the doctor's," he shouted over the noise.

I poked my head in through the open window and yelled in his ear, "Isn't Mrs. Ness coming?" For Helga stood there, hesitating. It seemed as if she wasn't sure what to do.

"Helga, come on now, we're waiting. We're going to need your help." She put her foot on the running board and swung into the cab alongside Mr. Percy.

My mother was out the back door, drying her hands on her apron, before we stopped.

"Glory be to God," was all she said when Mr. Percy told her about the boys. Back into the house she ran, grabbing her purse and hat. She stepped up and squeezed in beside Helga.

The truck couldn't go fast, but still the jolting caused Mike to groan as we clattered over loose planks of bridges and hit a few potholes. Jim was quiet. What if he were dead? I didn't know which was worse. To have one of them too quiet or to have one groaning in pain, but I knew it was going to be a long trip into Gibson's Landing to see Dr. Howard.

3

DR. HOWARD was in. We were in luck because he had the whole peninsula to take care of and sometimes was away all day.

"Thanks be to God," my mother murmured. The doctor took a quick look at Jim and Mike before he helped us move them into his treatment room.

Going to the foot of the stairs, he called up to his wife, "Mollie, could you come right away and give me a hand?"

Waiting only until Mollie had put on a white gown, Doc began to give orders. "Mollie, give Mike there in the X-ray room an eighth of a grain of morphine. Mother," he said to my mother, "you go and sit with the boy. Now you—Sheila, is it? You come over and watch. You may as well learn something while you're here."

He looked briefly at Jim's wound, then covered it with a sterile gauze. The fact that he could go on talking in that matter-of-fact way as he worked reassured me.

"We check the eyes of a head injury." And he thumbed up the lid of one. "See that pupil? Okay, now the other. Both seem to be the same size and normal. Okay, check the ears for bleeding...the nose...the mouth. This bothering you? No? Good girl. Hand me that blood pressure apparatus...the black box. And the stethoscope. Roll that sleeve up for me... higher. Blood pressure a little low, but that is to be expected. Get his shirt up out of the way. Let me hear his chest. Now, then, turn him on his side and hold him there."

He placed his stethoscope in several places on Jim's back, then went back and checked them all again. He looked thoughtful. Tucked a thermometer in Jim's armpit, waited a minute or so, whistled through his teeth. Held the thermometer to the light, stopped whistling.

"Mollie, you back yet? Put a dressing on his head wound and let Sheila see your sterile technique. We may have a future nurse here." He winked at me.

As soon as the X-rays of Mike's leg were dry, he held them up to the light. It was an uncomplicated break, he said, and Doc had me help him put a plaster of Paris cast on Mike's leg.

Then Doc sat down with my mother and talked to her about Jim. "I can't let him go home with you yet. He'll have to stay at least the night. He needs close attention. No, no…" He put his hand out to calm her. "I know you would watch over him carefully, but his blood pressure has to be taken every fifteen minutes, for one thing, and Mollie is trained to do that. It seems like only a concussion to me, but he is running a temperature and he has lost a lot of blood. Now I don't want you worrying. He's young and strong, and I'm quite certain he'll be right as rain. Do you have a phone?"

My mother shook her head. "The only one in the Landing is at the store."

"Mr. Percy still running the store?"

"Oh, yes."

"Then there's no problem. If I need to get in touch with you, Mr. Percy's my man. Now, why don't you phone me first thing in the morning, say around ten? I'll know better then how he is."

After we had settled Mike in the back of the truck and were ready to go, Doc had a few words for me.

"I've given your mother some 282s to give Mike for pain. Your job, Sheila, is to keep an eye on his foot. It should be a normal color. Not blue. He should be able to move his toes freely, and they should be warm to touch. Will you do that?"

Would I do that? At that point I would have done anything for Doc. He treated me as if I were a grownup. I loved him.

* * *

Home. Minus Jim. Mike on the kitchen couch, leg up on pillows, cast still cold and wet, but toes warm, pink and moving. My head back, slouched in a chair beside him. My brother Tom polishing his fishing spoons. All this had happened when he had been out fishing. My mother, Helga, and Mr. Percy finishing supper at the kitchen table. The sun, low in the sky, slanting in at the window, lighting on the polished kettle, my mother's wedding ring, and striking green-gold depths in the cat's eyes. The doctor's words, gestures, face, blending in and out of my drowsy head. Me in a white uniform, long hospital halls… My mother and Mr. Percy talking, Helga quiet as usual.

My mother got up to make fresh tea. Helga's eyes followed her, then strayed to Mike.

"How old is the boy?" Helga asked.

I sat up straighter. Other then telling me to get Mr. Percy at the beginning, they were the first words she had spoken all that long afternoon.

"Mike? Oh, he's ten. In March. He's in grade four," said my mother.

"And your girl?" Now her eyes were on me.

"Sheila's fifteen, sixteen at the end of June. She's just finishing grade eleven. It's her last year at school."

I couldn't believe I had heard her right. I stared at her across the room.

She stared right back.

"You don't have to go to school anymore, Sheila. It's only law that you go until you're fifteen." From the tone of her voice, she might have been talking about feeding the chickens.

"But I want to go to school!" I stood up, shaking.

"Well, we'll talk about it again," she said mildly. "It's not that you have to earn a living like the boys. You'll only end up married, with a family of your own."

A family of my own? Like her? That was the last thing I wanted. I wanted more than that. A career—maybe nursing.

"But I want—" I heard myself shouting.

"That will do, Sheila. We need another pail of water, please."

I grabbed the bucket and slammed out the door. Throwing the pail at the pump, I kept on going.

I went down to the beach and glowered at the mountains. They kept themselves blue, remote. I was so angry and shocked at what my mother had said that I bawled.

If Dad were here, he'd let me go to school. He'd want me to. Or Paul. He was proud of me doing well. Didn't he tell his friends, "My kid sister's the one with the brains in the family. She's the one brings home all the A's."

I was going to go to school. I'd never get away from here and be someone unless I did.

I don't know how long Helga had been sitting on the next log. I only know that when I had cried myself out, there she was. Sitting there, running shoes planted in the sand, bony knees, shapeless sweater.

She didn't say anything. The sun was setting. Keats Island was the last to go into the shadows. The tide was full, the water calm.

We sat a little longer. Then we walked back up the beach trail together.

4

I PUT OFF the talk with my mother about school. She was full of concern about Jim, and it seemed better to wait.

The next morning we went to the store to use the phone. Mr. Percy led us back to the storeroom that was between the store proper and the post office. It was stacked with cases of Pacific canned milk, pork and beans, pears; cartons of toilet paper, soap flakes, crackers, gunny sacks of potatoes. The phone was black and hand-cranked, and set up on the wall.

Even if Mr. Percy had wanted to avoid hearing the conversation, he couldn't have. He was making out an order for supplies, and I watched him count, then jot down items on the order sheet.

We could hear my mother. "Yes...yes...but..." Her voice rose in agitation.

Mr. Percy stopped writing. When my mother rang off, up went those eyebrows of his, and he asked, "How is the boy?"

My mother worked at her lip nervously. "The doctor said Jim has pneumonia. He isn't conscious yet. They want to try some new drug—penicillin." She rubbed at her eyebrows. "I don't know what to think, I'm sure." For the first time, I thought my mother looked old. Her face was drawn, and there were deep lines running down from her nose to both sides of her mouth.

Mr. Percy patted her shoulder. "Not to worry. I know all about this penicillin. They're calling it the wonder drug of the century. They say it's saved thousands of our boys overseas. Now you stop fretting, Mrs. Brary. After I close up today, I'll pick you up and drive you over to Gibson's. Wouldn't be a bit surprised if we find Jim much better. Yes, even in that short a time. I tell you, this is a miracle drug. Read all about it in *Life*." And so, patting and consoling, encouraging and commenting, Mr. Percy sent us on our way, feeling hopeful.

* * *

By afternoon the house was swept and dusted, and the washing hung on the clothesline where it billowed out in the ocean breeze. Finally I was free to visit Sonia.

I hadn't seen her since the night of the basketball game

at Port Mellon. There was so much I wanted to tell her—about Jim and Mike, Doc Howard and Helga...

But when I got to the Kolosky house, I found it in an uproar. There were mattresses hanging from the windows, blankets airing on lines, smoke billowing from both chimneys. Children ran everywhere with stacks of clothing, school books, toys. In the middle of the turmoil stood Mrs. Kolosky, the baby straddled on one of her hips, while she directed traffic and gave orders. Mr. Kolosky had appeared mysteriously, and was loading furniture onto a pickup truck. He didn't look like a Kolosky. He was skinny and dark and had wisps of brownish hair showing from under the edges of his cap.

Sonia caught sight of me as she hurried by with a load of flattened tin cans for the pit at the back of their property. I helped her bury them, and all the while we talked.

"Guess what?" she said excitedly. "We're moving, and were going to have fourteen fruit trees and a hundred chickens!"

"You aren't moving far, are you?" I asked anxiously.

"To the Fraser Valley..." Her voice trailed off. It was too far for two fifteen-year-olds, and we both knew it. "We can write each other," she offered as comfort.

"It won't be the same," I managed to say, although my throat had tightened up, and I could feel the tears behind my eyes.

"No," she agreed, looking as though she wanted to cry, too.

We finished burying the cans in silence and walked back slowly to the house.

"I won't stay today. I'll only be in the way," I said. "When are you going?"

"This afternoon's boat."

"You can't," I said and couldn't stop the tears. Sonia put her arms around me, and we bawled together like two calves.

I saw the Kolosky family off on the afternoon boat. Sonia and I waved goodbye until the boat had rounded the point and all that was left was black smoke trailing from the funnels. The boat whistled then for its next call, Gibson's Landing, and its plaintive sound echoed and re-echoed from the mountains and in my head.

* * *

Mr. Percy called for my mother just as we had finished supper. My mother was ready—hat squarely on her head and purse in hand. She left me a list of instructions, and I could tell by the set of her mouth that she expected them all to be done.

"Oh, just a minute, Mrs. Brary," said Mr. Percy as he turned back to his truck. "I brought your mail over. Thought you'd want it. Letter for you, too, Sheila."

It was a letter from Bob McLean. There was his name and address in the upper left-hand corner of the envelope.

Before my mother could ask me who the letter was from, Mr. Percy handed her a pale blue airmail envelope.

"It's from your son, Paul. Go ahead, read it. We've got all the time in the world." He followed her into the kitchen.

My mother opened the letter carefully with a clean knife and read parts of it aloud:

...glad the war is over, in Europe at least... unsure of future plans, have been thinking seriously of going to university, under the government's grant to veterans...saw Dad in Halifax last week. He looked fine, but has no plans yet on what he is going to do after discharge...I have two weeks leave coming so should be home soon, probably around the middle of June.

Love to all,

Paul

Mr. Percy beamed at my mother. The lines in her face had smoothed out, and with a deep sigh she carefully placed Paul's letter in her purse.

"This is good news," she said. Even her voice was brighter. "Tom," she called to my brother who was doing his homework in the boys' bedroom, "why don't you come with us?" Turning to Mr. Percy, she asked, "Is that all right with you? If Jim's conscious, pray God, it'll do him the world of good to see Tom. He just worships his brother."

And so the three of them drove away, my mother's velvet hat glowing blue between Mr. Percy and Tom.

I read Bob McLean's letter:

Dear Sheila,

Can hardly wait to see you again. Please let me know if it's all right with your parents if I come down this weekend.

Love,

Bob

P.S. You have beautiful eyes.

How could I explain to him that even Sonia had never visited our house? My mother discouraged visitors.

"It's better to keep ourselves to ourselves," she said.

I picked up the stove lid lifter and dropped Bob's letter into the glowing remainders of the supper fire.

No letter from Dad. It had been more than a month since we'd heard from him. His last letter was stuck behind the kitchen clock, and I reached up to the small shelf where it was.

It was written from Halifax. I reread the words slowly, thinking maybe I could write him. Did I dare tell him about quitting school? What if my mother found out? If I were very careful about the way I wrote it...

I could mail it the next day. I had some stamps of my own.

Quickly working through my mother's list of chores, I made the porridge for breakfast and put water on to heat for bedtime washes. Then I washed and dried the supper dishes and put them away on the curtained shelves.

As soon as everything was done, I sat down at the

kitchen table and wrote to my dad. I tried to be as brief as possible: …Mom wants me to quit school…Jim and Mike were thrown from horses, and Dr. Howard let me help him. I think I would like to be a nurse, but that means finishing high school first…"

Finally it was written. I blew out the coal-oil lamp and, placing the envelope under my pillow, went to bed on the cot in the living room.

One advantage of sleeping in the living room was that I didn't miss out on anything. I heard the latest news from the radio in the kitchen. I knew when someone came in late or got up early.

The only times I didn't like it were when my mother and father quarreled. Then their voices rose and fell, and I couldn't block them out.

They had quarreled as far back as I could remember. Sometimes it was about money, other times about women my mother knew he was seeing. And always, the next morning, my mother would be angry. But she was afraid to show that anger to my father because he wouldn't have stood for it. And she didn't take it out on my brothers because they were boys.

Which left me.

As I'd grown older, I'd seen that she struck out at me because she couldn't strike out at anyone else.

5

WHEN JIM came home from Dr. Howard's, he looked pale and tired. He went directly from Mr. Percy's car to bed.

That evening I said I'd read to him if he wanted.

"Nothing mushy."

"How about *The Wind in the Willows*? You like the illustrations."

While we were looking at Moley and Rat in their blue-and-white boat, Jim looked up and asked, "Did you really save my life, Sheila?"

"Who said?"

"Dr. Howard. I heard him tell Mom."

"You did? What else did he say? Word for word!"

"I don't know! How do you expect me to remember?"

"Well, try!"

He gave an exaggerated sigh. "I can't remember." He screwed up his eyes, concentrating. "Something like, That daughter of yours is outstanding—or special—something like that. He said Mom must be proud of you."

"He said that?"

"Yeah, and how you stopped the bleeding and all that."

I whirled around and around the room, then stopped and hugged and kissed him.

"Mom!" he yelled. "Get Sheila outa here! She's kissin' me!"

I sailed out of his room. My mother looked up from the butter she had taken from the churn. Her hands were patting and molding the lumps into a mound. "Are you teasing him? Don't you have anything better to do?" I took my sweater from the nail at the back door. "What are you up to now?"

"Oh, nothing." I waved my hand airily and danced out the back door. Then I ran as fast as I could down to the beach.

The diving float had been anchored out for the summer, and I hopped onto its connecting float and raced to the end. I quickly peeled off my shoes and socks and sat dangling my feet in the phosphorescent water, kicking shining swaths of silver bubbles in the green-black sea.

The sky was still light, but the land had darkened into black shapes. Here, on the water below the sky, was where the world was now.

Leaning back on my arms, I looked up to count the stars. Only one.

"I wish, I wish…I want to go back to school."

* * *

Saturday morning I set the washtubs out on the bench in the sunshine. My mother came out with a full kettle of hot water to add to one of the tubs. She stood swinging the kettle in a nervous way as she watched me soap one of the boys' shirt collars. I wondered if she was going to ask me to make a thicker starch for the curtains, which lay in the bluing water.

"Sheila." Her voice had a tremor. "I'm going to buy some land."

I wasn't surprised. It was one of her dreams, and she'd often talked about it. Ever since I could remember, I had heard stories about the farm in Ireland—how it had been in the family for generations and how she knew every stone, every bush. When we lost our house in Edmonton during the Depression, because we couldn't pay the taxes, she'd cried as if there had been a death in the family.

"I have it all figured out," she said, taking from her apron pocket the used envelope she had written her calculations on. "I've got some money saved, Sheila. Helga Ness says she'll let me have the ten acres on this side of the creek for eight hundred dollars, two hundred down. It's a good buy."

She was excited, but I was too full of my own problems to listen.

"If you can buy the land, why can't I go to school, too?"

"Because you don't need to. You can get a job at Gibson's working at the bakery or something, and your pay check will help out at home."

"Why me? You don't expect Paul or Tom to do that. Why should I have to?" I turned back to the scrub board and began scrubbing with a vengeance.

"Because you're a girl."

What kind of an answer was that? I'd been hearing it all my life. You can't do it; you're just a girl. You can't have it; you're just a girl. It wasn't fair!

"If Dad were here—"

"But he's not, is he?" Flushed with anger, my mother stood rigid. Her shoulders were stiff and her back straight as a broom. I had gone too far. "And there's no telling when he will be. I gave up counting on your father long ago."

I knew it was useless to say any more. If Sonia were still around, at least there would be someone to talk to.

I tipped the wash water onto the vegetable garden and carefully wiped out the tubs before hanging them on the woodshed wall. I decided to go up to Sonia's old house.

She wouldn't be there, of course, but I wanted to sit on the Koloskys' steps again, to be by myself until I could think things out and calm down.

The gate was fastened tight. As soon as I put my hand on it, a dog started to bark. He was chained to the veranda, and he pulled and strained as if he wanted to break loose and come after me.

From the front door came two small children, followed by their thin, peevish-sounding mother. They all stared at me. Then a sullen, dark man appeared along the side of the house. He spoke sharply to the dog and came down the path toward me, the woman's eyes following him all the way.

"Do you want something?" His voice was surprisingly rich, with a lazy overtone. I found myself swaying slightly with its rhythm.

"Uh…no," I said, feeling fascinated and repelled at the same time. "I used to…Sonia was…you have any girls my age?"

At that his eyes became as sleepy as his voice, and he looked me over slowly and thoroughly. I felt too aware of myself. Somehow ashamed.

"No, none like you," he said. "Just little ones. Five and six."

"Robert!" came his wife's voice. It had the whine of a buzz saw. He smiled at me as though she were a joke between us, and I turned away in embarrassment.

I was glad to get away. This family was a mud puddle compared to the Koloskys. I stayed away after that.

* * *

The night my brother Paul was due home, the house was shining clean. We had his favorite foods ready for a late supper. His bed had been made up with sheets taken right from the clothesline, smelling of sun and sea. On the kitchen table, yellow-centered daisies sat snug in the old sugar bowl. Yellow linen napkins lay folded at each place.

The woodbox overflowed. There was enough kindling split to last the weekend, and the water pails stood full.

We were ready.

I went alone to meet the boat.

"What nonsense," my mother said. "Why should we go to meet the boat? We're here at home where we belong, and where he expects us to be. A little less show, Sheila, and a little more of what counts."

"But what counts, Mom?"

"What counts is being practical, not making a big show of things."

"To meet the boat?"

"Sheila, it could be late. It often is. There are more useful things you could be doing than hanging around the wharf. You and your father, you never give a second thought…"

The boat was late, but this only added to the festive air. Summer tourists had already started to invade the peninsula, and all along the beach was a string of cottage windows, glowing softly orange with coal-oil lamps. A smell of wood smoke hung in the air. I could hear the summer girls' silky laughs in the soft night and the young men's returning laughs, richer, deeper.

A long whistle sounded down the inlet, and the *Lady Cecilia* rounded the point. She looked like a ship out of a dream, soft lights flooding the waters around her, and I could hear muted music and scraps of conversation from the passengers.

She docked at the wharf in a sudden swirling of black waters into white. I caught the thrown headline and pulled its loop over the bollard. Then Mr. Percy took the spring and stern lines and made them fast. The gangplank came rumbling over the side of the ship, and the passengers swarmed down it—loggers in their caulk-boots, pulp-mill workers, summer visitors, fishermen.

I strained to see Paul.

There he was! Twenty-one, tall in his pilot's uniform— my handsome brother. Jumping up and down, I called to him, "Paul! Paul! Here!"

As soon as he was down the gangplank, he swung me up and around in a circle.

I wanted to show him off to everyone.

"Hey, Mr. Percy! Paul's home!"

As we went up the wharf, people stopped and clapped Paul on the shoulder, admired his wings insignia, and told him, "Mighty glad the war is over!" We turned off the wharf onto the beach trail, and home.

I saw Helga before he did. She was like a gray wraith flitting through the trees. It looked as if she was on one of her walks. She always seemed to just walk and walk...

As Paul and I walked home, I told him about Helga, and before long I found myself telling him about Mom wanting me to quit school. His mouth tightened, and I had a sudden rush of hope that perhaps he could persuade her to change her mind.

We could see our house now, and light shining through

the trees, and Paul began to whistle when we turned into our yard. The door opened and everyone came out on the porch. We all talked at once, it seemed. No one finished a sentence before someone else started a new one. We talked while we served supper, through the meal, and while we cleaned up.

Paul brought out presents for all of us from his duffle bag. Mine was a locket bracelet made of soft yellow gold.

It was after midnight before my mother noticed the time. "Sheila, Tom, Jim, Mike. Off to bed," she ordered as she poured another cup of tea for Paul and herself.

Their voices came seeping into the living room as I was going to sleep, my mother's rushing along with plans to buy the land and build a house.

Then I heard Paul's deeper one questioning, "Sheila... quitting school?"

I got out of bed quickly and went over to the living-room door to listen. Their voices came clearly down the hall.

My mother sounded annoyed.

"Helga refuses to sell the land unless Sheila can go to school. Why should she make it her business... Well, all I can say is she's not quite right in the head. But it is a beautiful piece of property. There's even some first-growth fir. And to have the creek! I'll never get another chance like this. Sheila's not to know about Helga's part in this—"

"Does Sheila know she's going back to school next year?"

"No, and I'm in no hurry to tell her. That girl is getting

harder to manage all the time. You've no idea how difficult she can be. I swear she's more trouble than all you boys put together. Just like her father. She's the same through and through. Selfish…"

I had heard all that before, and I stepped silently back over the cold floor and to bed.

I could stay at school! Oh, Helga!

6

DAD MUST HAVE written the day he got my letter. It was just a short note, really, about the weather, what he was doing, indefinite plans for the future—and a P.S. "Don't worry about school, honey. Something's bound to turn up."

My mother didn't say anything to me about school, either. Paul started to tell me in a roundabout way, but I told him I had overheard everything.

"Okay, then," he said. "You can stop worrying about that."

About a week after Paul's homecoming, my mother went into Vancouver to see a lawyer about transferring the Ness land title to her name. I went down to the boat to see her off, and after the *Lady Pam* had pulled out, I was surprised when Robert came over to talk to me.

I hadn't been back to the Kolosky house since that first day I'd met Robert and his family, and I had only said hello if I had to.

He asked me to baby-sit that night. He said he and his wife were going to the Legion dance at Gibson's, and could I come at about eight?

I had never baby-sat before, and since my mother had gone to Vancouver, I couldn't check it out with her. But I needed the money for a dress for the end-of-the-year school dance, so I said yes.

That night it rained and blew. The wind was fierce and building all the time. I was chilled and soaked by the time I got to the house on the Upper Road.

There was only the light on in the kitchen at the back. If I hadn't known the place so well I would have had trouble finding my way. The dog was tied up to the veranda rail, and he barked and snapped at me when I approached.

The back door opened. It was Robert.

"Come on in." Taking my jacket, he hung it behind the oil stove. "Sit down at the table and I'll get you some coffee. Get you warmed up."

The table was set with two cups and two plates and a cake in its baking pan. There was no sign of anyone else.

"Go ahead, have some cake. I baked it especially for you." And he poured coffee for both of us.

The light from the coal-oil lamp pooled around the table, leaving the area beyond in darkness. I was no longer sure where the door was. There was a heaviness in the air, maybe from the smell of diesel oil on Robert's clothing or from the heat of the stove.

"Where's your wife?" I asked him.

"Oh, she isn't quite ready yet," he answered easily, and I felt the perspiration break out on my back.

"Could you show me where the kids are, so I can check on them? When you're gone." I started to get up from the table. I had to keep my legs stiff to stop their trembling.

"Well, now, just a minute. They aren't here at the moment. The wife and kiddies are visiting the McDougals up the road. They'll be back soon. Relax. Sit down. Tell me about school."

He passed the cake to me. I saw that he had only the last two fingers on that hand. He saw me staring.

"It was an accident at Port Mellon," he said, watching my eyes.

I took a piece of cake and began to eat it slowly. Outside I could hear the fury of the wind as it slammed itself toward the open sea.

"I always wanted a chance to talk to you," he said. "It's good we have this chance alone."

The cake stuck at the back of my throat, and I got up to get a drink of water at the sink. I ran the tap and reached for my jacket.

Instantly he was at my side, his hand with the missing fingers on my arm. "Where are you going? I told you they would be back soon."

"I know." I located the kitchen door in my mind. "I

think I'll go up to the McDougals. Remind them of the time. Maybe they—"

The vacuousness left his face, and he became heavy-lidded, full-lipped. His voice was very soft and wrapped itself around me.

"They're not there," he said. "They went into the city on the same boat as your mother. Stay and talk to me. We've never had a chance to talk, you and I. There are things I want to tell you."

I had my hand on the doorknob by this time.

"No!" I cried out when he lunged for me, and I pulled open the door and hurled myself into the blackness outside.

I was off the veranda and onto the path by the time he got out the door. I heard him shouting, swearing. Then he went back into the house, reappearing almost immediately with a powerful flashlight. The beams came down the path after me, and I veered sharply off the road and into the tangle of the garden. Blackberry vines caught at my clothing and ripped my face.

Tearing my way through them, I cut across the property toward the road. The light played up and down the path.

I reached the road and started to run. The wind was a wall coming at me. Trees creaked all around. All I cared about was running, running until I was sure he was far behind me.

By the time I was near home, I had a stitch in my side and was limping.

Everyone was in bed, even Paul. He looked up at me through the open door.

"You're back early. Did they change their minds?"

I stepped into the bedroom. He looked at the torn clothing, the rips on my face, the mud on my knee.

"What happened?"

I told him. He got out of bed and pulled his clothes on over his pajamas. Put on a jacket. Got a flashlight.

"What are you going to do?" I asked him.

"I'm going to take care of him. He's going to find out he can't do that to my sister and get away with it."

I was horrified.

"No, don't do that! He's really...scary." But Paul wouldn't change his mind.

After he had gone and I had cleaned myself up, I went to bed.

So this was what it was like having a man defend you.

My dad had been away now for five years—except for brief leaves—and I had forgotten the feeling of having a man in the house.

Paul came in about an hour later. His footsteps sounded slow and heavy. He blew out the lamp in the kitchen and went to bed without a word. I heard the sound of his boots drop to the floor.

I lay there listening to waves pound on the beach below the house, and the wind lift the shingles on the cottage.

Why didn't Paul say something?

"Paul?"

"Yeah."

"What happened?"

"Nothing. Go to sleep."

"Did you...have a fight?"

"No. Now will you quit bothering me and go to sleep?"

"What do you mean, go to sleep? An hour ago, you're mad at him. Now that you're home, you seem mad at me!"

No answer.

"Paul! Tell me! What's the matter? Why won't you tell me? Did he say something?"

Another long silence. Then, just when I thought he wasn't going to say anything more about it, his voice came, harsh and flat.

"He said you had been asking for it ever since he moved here, and how was he to know you didn't mean it?"

I couldn't reply. There were no words. I knew, instinctively, that there was nothing I could say to defend myself.

The wind shifted and rattled down the chimney. One of my younger brothers turned in bed, knocking his arm against the wall. The rain lessened to the gentlest of sounds. From the boys' bedroom I heard Paul's breathing deepen, become slow, regular. He slept.

I was emptied, hollowed out, conscious of feeling a profound loss. I sensed that there existed in the world a mysterious banding together of men. Against women? Whatever—I was outside it. And there was nothing I could do but lie there and stare, uncomprehending, into the darkness.

7

MY MOTHER came back from Vancouver two days later with the land title in her purse.

"It's registered in my name only," she told Paul late that night when the rest of us were in bed. "Your father won't be able to touch it."

Then Paul said something that shocked me.

"Did you ever think of divorcing him?" Since joining the air force, he had started to smoke, and the smell of his cigarette drifted into the living room where I lay, no longer sleepy.

I strained to hear my mother's answer. Her voice sounded pleased. She seemed to welcome Paul's concern. Yet there was something else in it—a pride, a falseness.

"Oh, no, the Church doesn't believe in divorce. You know that. A promise is a promise."

"But you haven't been happy with Dad for years. At least with a divorce you'd be free of him."

I heard the stove lid lift and a piece of wood being dropped into the fire box. "Free? I'll never be free of him."

"What do you mean?"

"I mean when you love somebody, you stay. Hoping for the best. The first time I set eyes on your father, I knew he'd be trouble for me. And yet I couldn't seem to help myself."

A smell of freshly perked coffee and the sharp, sweet scent of cinnamon toast made me hungry. I had questions I wanted to ask, too. But I knew if I got up and went out to the kitchen, my mother would be angry. There were times when she liked to talk to Paul alone, as if he were the only adult she could confide in.

And the right time for questioning my mother about love—and how it could make you so unhappy—didn't come.

For one thing she was studying house plans. Mr. Percy had given her the latest issues of several magazines that featured house plans. Each evening, as soon as supper was cleared away, she and Paul and Tom went over the magazines, trying to decide on the house they wanted.

My mother wanted three bedrooms. Paul insisted that there be electricity. Tom wanted to have an upstairs.

At last they decided on a three-bedroom bungalow, wired for electricity and provision made for developing the attic and a bathroom at some time in the future.

The coupon for ordering the blueprints was clipped,

and along with a money order for twenty-five dollars, bought from Mr. Percy at the post office, it was sent to the magazine. Within two weeks the blueprints arrived, and I was elated when Paul pointed out a bedroom for me at the back of the house.

One day all of us walked over to the land to choose the best site for the new house. The late June sunlight made the woods a pattern of shifting shadows, and great yellow shafts of light beamed from the treetops to the forest floor. Near the creek we found a level area thick and heavy with meadow grass. The grassy clearing was ringed with dark glossy cedars, and through them we saw blue glimpses of the sea. Like soft music in the background, creek water ran over mountain rocks.

"It's perfect," my mother said.

After the bulldozer cleared a way from the main road to the building site, lumber began to arrive by the truckload. There were cedar posts, beams, joists, two-by-fours, windows and bundles of cedar shingles held together with wire. None of the lumber was finished. It all had to be planed by hand.

Paul and Tom were up and ready to work as soon as it was light in the morning. When I saw the progress made on the house each day, I could hardly believe that my brothers had done it themselves.

My mother and I did a lot of extra baking. The boys were always hungry. And we always had kettles of hot water ready for them to wash off the day's dirt when they came in at dusk.

My younger brothers, Jim and Mike, took care of the water and wood supply for the household. My mother, besides taking care of the cow and chickens, had started to dig a shallow trench for the water pipes to the house. Sometimes at night her arms were so stiff that she couldn't take out the hairpins that kept her black hair in a neat roll at the back, and she called me to help. She sat, hands relaxed in her lap, a smile softening her face as she told me how Pep, our dog, had worked right along with her, his paws digging beside her shovel.

The new house never seemed to belong to me in the same way it belonged to my mother and brothers. Maybe it was because I was away eight or nine hours a day, working at a summer job.

It was Mr. Percy, really, who had got me the job. Jobs weren't all that plentiful for someone my age. When the Lawsons from Vancouver had inquired at the store for a girl to help out for the summer, Mr. Percy had recommended me.

The Lawsons had a cottage right on the beach near the diving float. It was one of the newer, more modern ones made of wood and glass, the sundeck gay with red-and-white chaise lounges and flower boxes of white-and-red petunias.

Mrs. Lawson was in her early forties, her blonde hair done in broad waves standing out from her head. She was only a few years younger than my mother, but they were very different. Although Mrs. Lawson always seemed to be smiling, her smile didn't make it to her eyes. They were dark blue, with a black outer ring around the iris, and there was no expression in them. Not like my mother's eyes. When she smiled, her eyes were candle flames, and when she was unhappy, their depths were sad songs. Other times they could snap and glitter green.

I tried to describe Mrs. Lawson to my mother when we were doing the dishes together after supper.

"Right after breakfast she goes into the bathroom, and she stays there for an hour and a half, maybe two hours. She washes her hair and has a bath, puts on lipstick and powder and rouge—even mascara. Every day she does her nails a new color. Once it was purplish. It's called Hot Grape."

"You're making that up."

"No, honestly! That's what it's called. Hot Grape."

"I guess she looks beautiful, then—her hands and all," my mother said almost wistfully.

I was astonished. "I thought you'd think it was terrible of her to be that vain."

My mother set down the dish towel and looked at her own hands, turning them over and back. "People used to say, when I was young, that I had beautiful hands. I did, too, even if I shouldn't say so myself. I kept the nails buffed and looking nice all the time. Look at them now."

I looked at her hands. They were rough, calloused. One nail was violet where she had missed with the hammer.

"I think you have beautiful hands, Mom."

When I said that, she sighed and picked up the dish

towel, and I wished I could say the right thing for once. It seemed I lacked the knack to please her.

"What about Mr. Lawson and their boy? What are they like?" She returned a fork that was still dirty to my dishpan of suds.

I worked away at the offending dried gravy on the fork. "Mr. Lawson's okay, I guess. Mild, sort of. George is quiet. Almost a sissy."

"How old is he?"

"Six. Mrs. Lawson doesn't like him to play too hard. She makes him lie down after meals for an hour, things like that. She's always taking his temperature and giving him vitamins."

"What's the matter? Is he sick?"

"No, that's just the way she is. Fussy."

"Too fussy by far," declared my mother.

"The pay's good, though." Fifty cents an hour and lunch. I moved over to wipe off the oilcloth.

"True. It will come in handy for your books and things for school next year."

My back was to her when she said this, and I was thankful. I spoke carefully. "Does that mean I'll be going into grade twelve after all?"

"Oh, I think so," she said matter-of-factly. "Mind you, I want you to get a part-time job—after school, or at least on the weekends—to help out."

"Okay," I said, not trusting myself to say more.

We finished tidying up the kitchen in silence.

* * *

Paul's month-long leave from the air force came to an end. He was to report to the base at Gander Bay. Before he left he made arrangements to have a carpenter and his son come in and finish the house. The Bergstroms were new arrivals in Gibson's Landing, and Tom was going to work with them.

My first sight of Nels Bergstrom was of him laughing at something his father had said. His head was thrown back, his shirt was open at the throat, and I could only stare.

Paul introduced us. "Nels, this is my sister, Sheila."

"Hi," he said and turned back to his work.

From then on I tried everything I could think of to make him notice me. Mrs. Lawson took me into Vancouver with her one weekend to get their city house in order, and while I was there I went to the hairdresser and had a feather-cut. Everyone was having one that summer. It made my hair seem thicker and darker, and I looked older, I thought. That and a new sharkskin blouse, white sandals and a pair of yellow shorts that could be rolled high on the leg, plus a tube of Tangee Natural lipstick—all bought at Woodward's with my first pay check, just before we caught the Union steamship home.

I hoped Nels would pay attention to me now.

My brothers didn't help matters. The first afternoon I stopped by on my way home from work, wearing my new shorts and blouse, I heard Tom shout, "Oh, boy! Watch out, Nels! Here comes your girlfriend!"

Jim, who was putting up shelves, called out, "Hey, Nels, did you know Sheila shaved her legs?"

"You creep!" I told him that evening when I knew my mother was outside, closing the chickens in for the night. "You'd better not do that again!"

"Or what?"

"You'll be sorry!" I tried to put as much threat as I could into my voice.

But none of it made any difference. Nels ignored me completely. And so after a couple of weeks I gave up and pretended I didn't care about Nels Bergstrom at all.

8

───────────
───────────
───────────

MY BIRTHDAY CAME. Sixteen at last. Here I was, aching to have a boyfriend, and what did I have? There was Bob McLean at Port Mellon who never wrote again, and Nels, who thought I was just a kid.

I began to pay more attention to the boys who were up for the summer, the cottagers from the city. The summer before, I had had a paper route, and after collecting the newspapers off the late Friday night boat, I would sit on the grassy bank above the community hall and watch the couples dancing. I longed to be part of their magical world, but the dances were for the summer boys and girls. It was their record player that was used, and they owned all the records—Glenn Miller, Benny Goodman, Tommy Dorsey, Charlie Spivak.

I knew I didn't belong. Not then, not now. Not even in the way I dressed. I wore slacks and blouses and sweaters that had been ordered from Eaton's catalogue. Their clothes looked special, somehow. There was a craze for V-neck sweaters, the longer the better. Some of them were long enough to reach below the hips. All through the summer the girls sat on the village-store veranda knitting away at their sweaters. I heard one of them say she was working on her seventh one.

In every way, it was a summer of excesses. My family was busy all the time, my mother too involved with the progress of the house to pay any attention to me. I could have gone out every night with Nels if he'd asked me. Blackberries dragged down the bushes with their heavy, swollen clusters. More salmon were caught than ever before. The days were hotter, the ocean saltier, the nights softer, the music sweeter.

I saw Helga every day. From the Lawsons' many windows I had a good view of the beach and the diving float, and I often saw Helga come down the path to the beach, the same shapeless print dress flapping against her thin brown legs. Her feet were bare, and as a further concession to summer she wore a peaked fishing cap, faded blue. Her skin was brown and wrinkled, like walnut meat.

She spent whole days away, off by herself, somewhere in her boat.

I asked Mr. Percy about it when I shopped for the Lawsons' groceries. He told me that every summer Helga took her boat out and searched the bays and rivers. She went as far up as Port Mellon and right out to the mouth of the Sound.

Was she still looking for her sons, I wondered?

"Leave her be," Mr. Percy said. "She's working things out her own way."

* * *

Mrs. Lawson liked things perfect. I think that was her problem—trying to be a perfect mother, keep a perfect house.

It was hard to please her. George began to wet his bed from time to time, which threw Mrs. Lawson into a frenzy. That in turn drove Mr. Lawson into having two drinks before dinner.

One of my jobs was the family laundry, and I knew things weren't quite right for Mr. Lawson when I came to wash his pajamas. After I had soaked them and placed them on the scrub board, rubbing the bar of Sunlight soap over the crotch area, I felt a diffusion of mucus. It came up in my hand like egg white. The smell reminded me of bleach. It took me a few minutes to figure out what it could be.

At school I had heard about wet dreams, but until now I thought only young boys had them.

One morning Mr. Lawson followed me into the utility room, a cup of coffee in his hand and his freshly shaven face bland and pink above his cardigan sweater. He watched me scrubbing George's sheets.

"How is it you're doing the washing, Sheila?"

"I always do it."

"Mrs. Lawson used to send it to town."

"I've done it ever since I started here."

He swirled the coffee back and forth in his cup.

"I'll see that it gets sent into Vancouver from now on. I don't want to see you doing it." He reached out as if to pat my shoulder but dropped his hand on my breast instead.

I moved quickly away. I felt shamed.

First Robert. Now him.

After that I kept alert when Mr. Lawson was around. Otherwise I risked feeling his quick hand on me.

* * *

One late afternoon as I was making a potato salad for supper—or dinner, as Mrs. Lawson called it—I saw, through the window, Helga tying up her boat at the diving float. Mr. Lawson lay spread-eagled on one of the chaise lounges, his eyes closed and his mouth slightly open. Mrs. Lawson's chair was next to his. She flipped restlessly through the latest *Vogue*. George was sitting alone on the beach, watching the other boys jump and belly-flop from the diving board. "No swimming today, George," his mother had told him. "I heard you coughing during the night."

It was a brassy, hot July day. The sun was too bright, and everywhere lights glanced and bounced off reflecting surfaces. The world shimmered and hurt the eyes. It even smelled hot—sweet and dry.

Helga looked exhausted when she straightened up from her boat. She dragged her feet along the float and stumbled, almost falling when she reached the beach. I watched her ease herself down off the float and sit on a log.

Quickly I filled a glass with water to take to her, but I had no sooner got out the door and down the steps when she got up slowly and moved toward George.

She stared at him for a minute. He did look pathetic, sitting hunched up in a too-warm sweater and long corduroy pants. She put her hand out hesitantly and touched the top of his head lightly.

He looked up at her.

"What's the matter, boy?" I heard her ask him.

"What are you doing? Leave him alone!" It was Mrs. Lawson shouting at Helga. She knocked over the chaise lounge in her hurry to get to George. I felt as though the brittle afternoon had broken into a thousand sharp pieces.

Helga took one look at Mrs. Lawson's face and bolted for the trail in the woods.

By the time Mrs. Lawson had got George into the house, she was almost hysterical. I found myself giving her the glass of water I had brought for Helga.

"That crazy old woman," she kept saying over and over. Her husband tried to calm her, but she pushed him aside angrily. "You've got to do something about her," she told him. "I mean it!"

When I left for the day, she was still going on about

Helga. I stopped at the store on my way home to tell Mr. Percy about it.

"I'm sure she's going to make trouble for Helga. She was even talking about going to the other summer people and getting a petition or something. She says Helga's frightening the children and ruining the place for the cottagers."

Mr. Percy shook his head, exasperated.

"That Mrs. Lawson, she would, too. She's just the type. And once she gets a notion in her head, there's no stopping her. If she had her way, all the male dogs in town would be wearing underwear."

"Is that why—?"

"Eh? Why what?" Mr. Percy demanded.

"Mr. Lawson. He's always...he's got roving hands."

Mr. Percy's eyes chilled. They stared hard into mine.

"Oh, has he, now? That's what I call interesting. Yes, sir, real interesting."

When I left, he was looking thoughtful.

* * *

The annual regatta was coming up in a few days, and Nels and Mr. Bergstrom constructed the judges' platform. Everyone was busy putting up banners and decorating the wharf with paper roses and twisted streamers.

Everybody, that is, except Mrs. Lawson. She was too busy talking to people about Helga.

I saw her in the middle of a group of women at the beach, gesturing angrily. She invited them into the house for tea and cookies, and from the kitchen where I was iron-ing George's shirts, I overheard bits and pieces of their con-versation—enough to tell me that Helga was in trouble.

On the day of the regatta I was given the afternoon off so that I could go to the beach and watch. Everyone was there: Nels and his father, my brothers. My mother had said she would come, but at the last minute she changed her mind. Mr. Percy was out on the store's veranda, and I saw Mrs. Lawson leave her husband's side and go to speak to him. I guessed it must be about Helga. That was all she talked about those days.

Then I did something that I didn't consciously plan. Acting out of an impulse that suddenly hardened into a resolve, I moved over so that I stood in front of Mr. Lawson. Mr. Percy and Mrs. Lawson were still talking, but their heads were turned in my direction.

I leaned back toward Mr. Lawson as provocatively as I could. His hand reached around and cupped one of my breasts, briefly. It was only for a moment, but I could tell, by the fixed look on Mrs. Lawson's face, that she had seen.

But so had Nels Bergstrom, who was leaning against the barrels at the head of the wharf. Now, of all times, he saw me.

* * *

I was afraid to go to work the next morning. I didn't know whether Mrs. Lawson would refuse to answer the door, or fire me on the spot.

But it was as if nothing had happened. There was no

yesterday with Mrs. Lawson, no hint of approval or disapproval in her eyes. If anything, she appeared more regal—standing straighter, her blonde hair more sculptured than ever. As for Mr. Lawson, he ignored me, and I did the same to him.

For the first few days after the regatta, I avoided our new house. I was afraid to face Nels. But I made up my mind to be like Mrs. Lawson—to pretend nothing had happened, and to look Nels Bergstrom right in the eye.

Walking down the grassy ruts of the new road to our house-to-be, the alder stumps on either side bleeding orange, I heard the staccato of hammering. Mr. Bergstrom and Tom were on the roof laying shingles. There was no sign of anyone else. I wandered through the rooms, smelling the fresh lumber, touching the clean yellow wood. Turning into what was to be my bedroom, I almost fell over Nels. He was on his hands and knees just inside the door, studying the blueprints.

"There's no closet," he said, sitting back on his heels.

"What?" Being so close to him without warning, I found it hard to think.

"The blueprints. Look. They forgot to leave room for a closet."

I bent over, as if I could read them upside down without any problem.

"Well, I want one. Couldn't you put one in anyway?"

"It'll stick out, even in a corner. I'd better check on it." He stood up abruptly.

We were standing too close. I moved over to the window.

I played with the catch, then slid the window back and forth. "You've put this in since I was here last. I like it."

"They're all right. A lot of work, though, making the casement and frames...How old are you, Sheila?" He finished rolling up the blueprints and put a rubber band around them.

"Sixteen. Why?"

He pushed his fingers through his dark hair in a gesture of annoyance. "Aren't you kind of young...to be fooling around?"

I felt my face flood hot and the warmth go down my neck.

"I mean, the guy was old enough to be your father. Who was he, anyway?"

"Since when is it any of your business?" I asked, humiliated that he would talk about it at all.

"Hey, calm down. I just don't like to see a kid like you being pawed over by some middle-aged man ..."

"It's not like you think."

"What is it, then?"

While Nels was talking, I couldn't look at him. Now I forced my eyes back from the window, and what I saw in his eyes was interest. I found myself telling him in a rush of words about wanting to go back to school, how Helga had made it possible, why Mrs. Lawson was making trouble for Helga. I told him everything.

"Do you think it worked with Mrs. Lawson?" he asked when I had finished.

"It seems to. She's so busy now being the perfect wife, she's stopped talking about Helga."

He stood there, half laughing at me, half serious.

"No wonder your brothers say one sister's enough." He leaned back with his hands on the window ledge and, still smiling, said, "So it's settled then."

"What's settled?"

"That you're going to the show with me on Friday night."

"I am?"

"Walter'll let me have the truck. I'll pick you up at seven-thirty. Don't be late."

"Walter?"

"Walter Bergstrom. My stepfather."

"I didn't know he was your stepfather."

"There's a lot about me you don't know, yet, but I'll tell you about it Friday night."

He left then to talk to his stepfather about the closet, and I walked home, almost in a daze but sensing every quiver of every leaf on every tree along the way. Even the birds seemed part of it. The woods were full of their singing.

* * *

Friday night. I heard Nels' truck turn into our yard, but he didn't come to the door. Instead he waited for me to come out, the motor running. I found myself wishing he would at least come to the door. What would my mother think? I felt apologetic when I told her, "That's Nels Bergstrom. He's taking me to the show."

She scarcely looked up from the bank statement she had been worrying about ever since it had come in the mail. The money she had saved for the house was almost gone, and the inside was yet to be finished, the insulation put in. "All right, Sheila, don't be late," was all she said. When I left, she was adding up the debit side of the figures once again.

Nels leaned over from behind the wheel and opened the passenger door. I climbed in beside him, careful to keep my white pleated skirt down in place at my knees.

It was impossible to talk above the noise of the truck on the gravel road. Once in a while Nels caught me looking at him. Then he smiled, and I was glad we couldn't talk—this was much easier.

He had on dark blue pants and a white cotton shirt open at the neck. He smelled of shaving soap and wood smoke and his own smell which came from his skin and hair.

The movie was shown in the Gibson's community hall. The films were always old, usually Westerns or B movies. I had vague impressions of cowboys on horses flickering on the screen, but I was really only conscious of Nels.

Several times the film broke. The projectionist, one of the elementary school teachers, tried to repair the damage while young boys lobbed water bombs through the air. One bomb landed with a plop near the projectionist, but he went on with his work, absently wiping off the water as he peered at the reels with a flashlight. There were yowlings of dogs fighting on the steps outside the side entrance, and in a sudden fury they landed against the door, springing it open. They fell inside the hall in a tangle of tails and snapping jaws. This made the small boys howl with glee and egg them on.

I looked around. There was a girl from school, and she waved at me and made an O with her mouth as if to say, Who's that? Nels pointed out his mother and stepfather who were sitting two rows ahead of us.

Mrs. Bergstrom looked very young to me, in her mid-thirties. Her hair was an unnatural shade of brown and done in ringlets, but only at the ends. It reminded me of Scarlett O'Hara in *Gone With the Wind*. She had on too much rouge.

"Isn't she beautiful?" Nels whispered to me, and I could only nod. "No one believes I'm her son, she looks so young."

The projectionist went on trying to fix the film while the older boys at the back of the hall made loud and insulting remarks. I could see that they were passing a bottle of Vat 69 back and forth.

"I want to say hello to my buddies," Nels told me, and he got up and went back to them.

When he sat down beside me ten minutes later, I could

smell the whiskey. He draped his arm over the back of my folding chair.

We never did see the end of the movie. The film had broken beyond repair. On the steps outside the hall afterwards, Nels stopped to talk to his friends. The bottle was passed around again.

"You wanna drink?" one of the boys asked me.

"No, she doesn't," Nels answered.

"Too young, eh?"

When we were back in the truck again, Nels said. "It isn't that you're too young, although you are. It's that I don't like to see a girl drink. Okay? I'll take you home."

We parked just this side of the road leading down to my house. Nels switched off the headlights. He lit a cigarette, and I could see his cheek bones and eyebrows in the quick flare of the match.

"Sorry." He shook the package toward me. "You want one?"

I took a cigarette and he struck another match. After I sputtered and coughed, he took the cigarette from my hand and stubbed it out in the ashtray.

"It helps," he said, "when it's a cork-tip, to smoke the right end. If you don't smoke, just say so. I don't like to see girls smoke, anyway." But he was smiling.

"There's a lot of things you don't like to see girls do. Drink, smoke, fool around."

"That's because they're cheap things to do. I don't like cheap girls. Girls who go around with any guy…"

"Well…thanks for the movie, anyway." I started to open the door.

He caught my arm and turned me toward him. "Don't be in such a hurry. I just wanted to make sure you understand. If you're going to go out with me, you don't go out with anybody else. And my girl doesn't act cheap."

I shook off his hand. "Nobody said I was going out with just you. And I don't act cheap, either. I've already explained about Mr. Lawson."

"Jesus, you're hard to get along with! All I'm trying to tell you is that if you're my girl, you've got to act like it."

"Who said I was your girl?" I could hear my voice rising.

He put his hand on the back of my head and kissed me slowly and gently.

"I said so."

And in a minute, after I had got my breath back, I answered, "Yes. All right." I opened the door and walked slowly toward the house. Nels put on the headlights and waited until I was at the door before he started the engine.

The house was in silence, the lamp turned low on the kitchen table. Everybody seemed to be in bed, although I could see by the kitchen clock that it wasn't even ten-thirty.

I could smell cigarette smoke. Something was different.

I went into the hall to the living room and could hear heavy snores coming from my mother's bedroom. And I could see, near the door of her room, an air force duffle bag.

My father was home.

9

I WOKE to the teasing smells of bacon frying and fresh coffee. From the kitchen I heard my father's voice, low and rambling, and my mother's answering monosyllables.

Slipping on a clean cotton dress for work at the Lawsons', I hurried out to see my father.

He looked different. It wasn't only the air-force blue shirt that made his face look ruddy. There was a hardness, a leanness that hadn't been there before. It showed in the slight tenseness of his shoulders as he sat, the sharp way he turned his head toward me.

Once I would have described him as easygoing. Now I wasn't sure.

"Sheila!" he said, opening his arms. "You're looking fine.

All grown up in a year. Sit down and tell me what you've been doing."

My mother set a plate of bacon, eggs and toast in front of him.

"When did you get home, Dad? How long can you stay?" I looked at his bacon. He picked up a slice, put it on a piece of toast and passed it to me.

My mother frowned. I took the bacon and returned the toast to his plate.

With his fork he broke the egg yolk.

"I've got a month's leave. The war's almost over, Toots. Any day now, and you'll see Japan surrender."

"What are you going to do then?" I wanted to know. My mother, who had just picked up the coffee pot from the stove, stopped, coffee pot suspended in the air.

"Oh, I'm not sure," he answered. "Probably go up north to the placer mines. Gold mining. Yes, that's where the money is." He pushed away his plate and reached in his shirt pocket for his cigarettes. My mother brought the coffee pot to the table and filled his cup carefully.

"Where would that be, Frank?" she asked, spooning three teaspoons of sugar into his coffee.

He stirred vigorously, slopping coffee in the saucer. "Around Williams Lake." He lit a cigarette, and my mother fetched him an ashtray. Relaxing, he leaned back in his chair and smoked.

My brothers came to the table for breakfast. The two younger boys threw themselves at Dad, who held them off at arm's length, pretending to be astonished at how they had grown. Tom stood, his grin joining his ears.

The boys were all talking at once—fishing, horses, the new house.

"New house? What new house?" My father leaned forward, suddenly alert.

"We were saving it as a surprise for you, Frank," my mother broke in, brushing the crumbs off the table into her hand. "I bought that piece of land on this side of the creek. Paul and Tom have built a house on it."

"Well, I'll say this is a surprise, all right. That's the understatement of the year." My father's face was mask-like, expressionless. Only the slightest hardness at the corners of his mouth showed how he really felt. "Where did you get the money for all this," and he waved his hand grandly, "land and new house?"

My mother's voice was quiet.

"I saved it from the family allotment checks from the air force." She moved to fill his coffee cup again, but he shook his head and covered the cup with his hand.

"That's mighty nice, Agnes. Not many women can manage a dollar the way you can. Gives a man a real sense of security to be a home owner again."

My mother began to clear the table. I moved to fill the basin with hot water to start the dishes.

"Jim and Mike are going to help me lay the water pipes today," she told my father, "as soon as I've tidied up here."

"You had no problem with the paper work? Everything's squared away in that direction?" His eyes were half shut, but I saw that he watched my mother closely.

She turned to face him.

"It's in my name, Frank, if that's what you want to know."

"Your name. Not even yours and mine?"

She didn't answer.

He got up then and walked around the room. Sat down. Sighed. Pushed the ashtray back and forth on the table.

"We'll see about that," was all he said.

As my mother stood beside me, drying the dishes, I saw the moisture on her upper lip. Her hand, as she hung up a cup, shook.

I dared to look at my father. He sat at the table, playing with the cigarette package. The clock ticked loudly in the silent kitchen.

"Oh, no! Quarter to eight!" I'd never make it on time to the Lawsons'.

"Wait," said my father. "I'll walk with you as far as the new house. I'd like to take a look at it. That is, if it's all right with your mother."

"Now, Frank, of course it's all right," she answered, almost successful in sounding brisk and cheery. "We could use your help. I'd hoped we could move in by the time school starts, but I don't know. There's so much to be done yet and the money all gone…"

She flung the dish towel toward its nail, missed, but didn't notice. She picked up her sweater from the kitchen couch and ran, with worried little steps, to catch up with my father, who was already out the back door.

I grabbed the dish towel and hung it where it belonged, then hurried after them.

* * *

We all worked hard on the house. My father did the wiring, and when it came to insulating, we all helped. We used blackout paper given to us by Mr. Percy, who had ordered too much of it at the beginning of the war. Nels and Mr. Bergstrom were paid and regretfully let go. The money had run out, and although my father was enthusiastic about the quality of their work, he didn't offer any money to keep them on the job.

Before Nels left, he made a closet for my bedroom. It was built on the narrowest wall, and he ran it across the whole width so that it didn't stick out.

One late afternoon Nels and I went swimming at the beach after work. He was a strong swimmer and stayed in long after I had tired. I dropped onto the hot sand, my skin tingling from the ocean. Now that it was mid-August, with its longer, colder nights, the water had a nip to it. I lay in the last of the afternoon sun, drowsy, completely content.

It made me shudder when Nels dribbled water from his hand onto my legs.

"You look too comfortable," he said. He sat down, his back against a log, and kept flicking me with water until finally I sat up beside him.

The sun was dropping behind Gower Point. I shivered. "Summer's almost over. School's in two weeks."

Nels wrapped a towel around my shoulder.

"I guess so. I never liked school myself. Quit in grade eight. Wasn't learning anything, anyway."

As we sat side by side, I could feel the length of his legs along mine. He began to gouge out the sand with his heels.

I pulled the towel tighter around me.

"I love school! And if I don't finish high school, I won't have a chance at a decent job. I'll end up working in a store or something."

He looked at me through wet eyelashes.

"What's the matter with that?"

"Well, nothing. It's… I want something more. I'd really like to go on to university. But at least I want to finish high school."

"It's never seemed that important to me." He slipped down to lie on his back, a towel rolled under his head for a pillow. "I've never been sorry I quit."

"Don't you miss learning about things? Reading?" Now I was making heel marks in the sand.

"Never. If I want to read, I read."

"What do you like to read?"

"Oh, I don't know. Westerns, mostly. Comic books, I guess."

I turned to look at him, thinking he must be joking. He pulled me down beside him.

"You're too serious, Sheila."

His body was warm beside me, and I had to close my

eyes against wanting him. He must have felt something, too, because his body tensed, and he turned over on his stomach, away from me.

That evening around nine, Nels' truck stopped outside our house. I heard only the short beep of a horn.

It was Tom who called to me, "Hey, Sheila, your boyfriend's waiting for you." My father looked up from his newspaper. He looked as if he wanted to say something, but I didn't wait to hear what it was.

I ran outside. Nels was smiling, pleased about something.

"I've got a surprise for you. Come on, get in."

We were at the new house in a matter of minutes. Taking me by the hand, he led me to the back of the house to my bedroom. There, under the window, was a desk. Not elaborate, but with a wide writing surface and shelves at one side for books and papers. It was made of fir and had been sanded, ready for the can of varnish that sat unopened on its surface.

"Well, how do you like it?" he asked, running his hands over its smoothness. "I came back after supper and made it for you. After what you said at the beach—about school."

"Oh, Nels! I love it! It's beautiful! I can't believe it—that you made it for me!"

"You really like it?"

I put my arms around him then. His long back felt hard under my hands.

"I love the desk, Nels. And…I love you."

His hands went to my hips. Pulling me into him so that

I could feel his warmth, he held me.

"I love you, too, Sheila."

* * *

On Saturday of the Labour Day weekend we moved into our new house, even though it wasn't finished inside. Black roofing paper had been spread over the floor until we could afford to put down a finished one. The inside walls were left with the two-by-fours showing.

"Handy for shelves," my mother said.

It had been my last day of work at the Lawsons'. George and his father were out fishing, so it was Mrs. Lawson who paid me. She gave me a five-dollar bonus, "for satisfactory work."

"I've enjoyed working for you," I said, and was surprised when I realized I meant it.

* * *

Sunday, September 2, 1945. Another day for the history books. It was VJ Day. The war with Japan was over. Since the middle of August we had heard that Japan had surrendered, but this was official.

My father turned up the volume on the radio as we sat eating our breakfast. The United States battleship *Missouri* was anchored in Tokyo Bay with General MacArthur on board, ready to meet with the Japanese.

As the radio gave out the news about VJ Day, I thought about meeting Helga on VE Day, and how upset she'd been when she heard the boat whistles and thought they meant her son and husband had been found.

"Mom, I'll do the dishes when I get back," I said, getting up from the table. "I've got to tell Mrs. Ness. About it being VJ Day."

There was a thin spiral of blue smoke coming from Helga's chimney. Otherwise there was no sign of life. As I knocked at the front door, I realized I'd never been inside her house, and some of my old fears came back, about her being crazy.

It seemed a long time before the door opened, and she held it so that it partially shielded her body.

"It's me, Mrs. Ness, Sheila Brary."

Her eyes were sharp, stared at me for what seemed minutes, then lost some of their fierceness. The door opened and she motioned me in.

Following her down the short hallway to the kitchen, I became conscious of the smell of apples, although it was a month too early for them. Did she store apples in her basement?

It came to me that Helga always smelled of apples.

The kitchen at the back of the house seemed bare and clean, maybe because it was uncluttered, unlike our kitchen which was always busy in some way. Either there was bread rising or butter being churned, a radio on, people talking, something bubbling on the stove or baking in the oven. Smells, movements, sounds.

Here in Helga's kitchen it was quiet.

We sat at her kitchen table. It was covered with a much-laundered cloth, vivid with embroidered flowers, and with a wide edging of crocheted lace. I ran the tip of my finger around the outline of a blue cornflower, then a sunflower with a dark-brown center.

Helga's eyes never left my face.

"You like some coffee?"

Without waiting for an answer, she brought over the speckled blue enamel coffee pot. There were clean mugs upside down on the middle of the table. I turned two of them over.

While we sipped at our coffee, I looked around. Dish towels, bright with cross-stitch, hung from a rod near the stove. By the back door was an oval hooked rug. Samplers hung on the wall. "Bless This House," "Home Is Where the Heart Is."

A breeze flapped the curtains over the sink. They, too, had bunches of flowers embroidered in bright colors.

"This morning we heard on the radio that Japan has surrendered," I said. "The war's over. People will be celebrating again, like last time. Do you remember? VE Day?"

"Ya-ah. I remember." Her eyes clouded with misery.

I couldn't help myself. I went over and gave her a hug. Her bony shoulders were like birds' wings under my hands.

10

═══════════

It was a beautiful September, an Indian summer month of mellow days and brilliant nights, when every star hung polished. The sea was a flat enamel blue, and the maple leaves showed yellow against a backdrop of hazy blue mountains.

As soon as we got off the school bus each afternoon, the boys and I dropped our books on the kitchen couch, changed into bathing suits and raced to the beach. Every day I thought, This will be the last swim of the year. By the middle of September I was numb with cold when I came out of the icy water, but the sun was hot and the air dry.

My father was based at Jericho Beach in Vancouver, waiting for his discharge from the air force. At first he came home every weekend. Then he announced, "I'll try to make it every other weekend. There are a few things I have to attend to in the city."

"A few things indeed," my mother told me, banging the pots. "A few women would be more like it. But the check coming in every month is the important thing. I've given up expecting your father to change."

My brothers missed Dad and told him so.

"You said you'd teach me to drive," Tom complained. "Besides," and he looked around to be sure my mother was out of hearing range, "I don't like Mom telling me what to do all the time."

"Who's running this house?" my mother demanded of the three of them at breakfast one morning. They had been slow getting in the wood and water, had dawdled over breakfast, and when she told them that the school bus would arrive at any minute, Tom, for no good reason that I could understand, refused to wear his old navy blue pants. My mother was furious when he came out wearing his new brown corduroy pair, but she had to let him. Either that or he would miss the bus.

"Times like this," she said savagely, "I wish your father were here to keep you boys in line."

To my surprise, I was relieved Dad wasn't home very much. He didn't like me going with Nels.

"You're much too young for that. Look at you running out to meet him! Like some common...he doesn't even have the decency to come to the door. What does he think of you? Eh? Answer me that! He must think you're not worth two cents!"

"That's not right! He feels…shy."

"Shy? I'll just bet he's shy! Till he gets you in that truck!" My father's eyes were all bloodshot, his face red. He had been drinking beer all afternoon. "But you like it, don't you?" He thrust his face close, and I could see the corner of one eyelid twitching.

"Dad! That's just…disgusting!"

It was the only time I'd ever talked back to him. He caught me by the wrist, then let my arm drop. His voice was so quiet I had to strain to hear.

"You ever speak to me like that again, and I'll beat you so that you'll never have children. You understand?"

I couldn't believe he had said the words. Didn't believe he could even think them. But I stared at the wall and said, "Yes." The kitchen clock ticked away like a bomb. "I'm sorry."

* * *

I was glad to be back at school. I had gained new status being Nels' girlfriend. The other girls went out of their way to talk to me, and the halls were filled with our chatter. Bookkeeping was being offered for the first time, and there was a rumor that our school might get three typewriters for a typing course after Christmas. I signed up again for the basketball team.

Dr. Howard and his wife Mollie came to the school to test our eyesight and check our teeth.

"Well, Sheila," Doc said, poking at my tonsils with the flat surface of a tongue depressor, "are those brothers of yours still riding horses?" I mumbled around the tongue depressor. "You're going to have to see a dentist soon. There are a few cavities starting." Doc swiveled around in his chair and noted it on my health card. "Ever think of taking a part-time job?" he asked, continuing to write.

"Well, I—"

"Mollie here and I would like to have a young girl come in Saturdays. Answer the telephone, give us a hand with dressings, that sort of thing. Would you like that?

The chair creaked. He turned back and waited for me to answer.

Would I like that? He took one look at my face and said, "Then it's settled. When would you like to start?"

* * *

There was no dentist on the peninsula, which meant going into Vancouver and staying overnight. My mother did not approve.

"Why do you have to get your teeth fixed, anyway?" she asked. "I lost all mine when I was thirteen because I had to drink an iron tonic. They said it was because I was so sickly. But it took all the enamel off my teeth, and they had to pull them all out. Why should it be any different for you?"

"But, Mom! That was Ireland, a long time ago. That doesn't happen anymore."

"I don't know where you get your ideas from," my

mother said, her voice angry. "You seem to think you deserve more than I did. I have no money to fix your teeth. You're too vain as it is, curling your hair, always looking in the mirror. Just like your father. Bad enough to have one of you in the household!"

But I had my own money to pay the dentist, and I was determined to go.

Nels didn't like the idea of me going to Vancouver and staying overnight at a hotel.

"Listen, Nels. I've got to go to the dentist. And there's no other way to do it." We had been to the Harvest Dance and had parked on the wharf at Gibson's to look at the harvest moon. I moved closer to him and touched his hand. "I'll be back on the Friday night boat. We can still go to the dance on Saturday night."

"I don't like it!" He sat well over on his side of the seat and put his arms up so that his elbows were resting on the steering wheel.

I moved back to my own side.

"What don't you like about it? I don't understand."

"Sixteen-year-old girls don't stay at hotels alone. Any guy finds out, you're in trouble."

He stared ahead at the wharf, ignoring the orange moon that had climbed high over the mountains on the mainland.

"Nels, you don't need to worry about me. After all, my father is going to get me the hotel room. Are you going to meet me when I come back? On the Friday night boat?"

"I don't know. Maybe I'll go to the show myself. Or take another girl."

"Oh, Nels!" I could see by the set of his jaw that he wasn't joking.

He turned the ignition key.

"I don't want to be made a sucker of, Sheila. Just don't forget that."

* * *

My mother still hadn't resigned herself to the fact that I was going to have my teeth taken care of. "You'd be better off to have all those teeth out, as I suggested. You'll be running back and forth to the dentist all the time. There will be no end to it."

"Do you want me to do any shopping in the city for you?" I asked, hoping to soften her mood.

"No...I suppose your father will be too busy to see you."

"He's getting the hotel room for me. He said we'd have supper together Thursday night."

She put her mending down and closed her eyes for a minute. Then she picked up another sock.

"Sheila, now you're not going to like this." She looked sharply at me. "But you need to know these things." She fitted the sock over the bottom of the glass she used for darning. "Don't let your father stay in your hotel room."

I stared at her, wondering what she was talking about.

"I mean it," she said, jabbing the needle at me. "There's

nothing—nothing—I'd put past him." She began to place small precise stitches along the edge of the hole in Jim's sock. "You needn't look at me that way! You think that never happens?"

Speechless, I reached for my science assignment. The workings of the internal combustion engine were easier to understand than what went on in our house.

Between Nels with his jealousy and my mother with her ugly warnings, I felt a sense of relief when at last I caught the boat into Vancouver the following Thursday. As soon as we'd left Gibson's and rounded Gower Point to the outside passage, I began to feel better. I was invited by the quartermaster for a mug-up in the mess room, and I was glad to go. There was a rich mixture of odors—fuel oil from the engine room, paint, rope, tar, sun, sweat.

"Are you doing anything tonight, Sheila?"

It was Jack, one of the deckhands. Somehow Jack and I were alone at the table. The rest of the crew must have drifted out. Jack was eighteen, had blond hair done in a ducktail and a smooth tanned chest showing at the V of his open shirt.

"Why?"

"I thought you might like to eat in Chinatown. Maybe go bowling."

"I don't know. My dad's supposed to meet the boat, and I don't know what he's planned."

"Should be finished here on the boat about six," Jack said, pouring canned milk into his coffee. "I could meet

you under the clock at Birk's at six-thirty." Even I knew
where the clock at Birk's was. "If you're not there by seven,
I'll know you can't make it. Okay?" He pulled at my hair
and flashed a smile on his way out.

My father was waiting for me when the *Lady Cecilia* tied
up at the Union pier at five-thirty that afternoon. He
looked younger than he had the last time I'd seen him, and
he had on a new jacket I'd never seen before. His shoes were
polished, and he smelled of after-shave lotion. But he was
preoccupied and in a hurry, as if he wanted to take care of
me as quickly as possible and be on his way.

We took a taxi—an unheard-of extravagance—to the
King George Hotel on Granville Street. He introduced me
to Murray, the desk clerk, as his "little girl."

I saw Murray give me a quick once-over. The thought
even came to me that Murray didn't believe my father. That
made me stop and make a point of talking to him about my
brothers and school and why I was in Vancouver.

Finally my father interrupted, "Sorry, honey, I've got to
run. You'll be all right, won't you? Got enough money?" He
was keyed up, jingling the loose change in his pocket.

"Sure, Dad."

I sensed his relief when he hurried away. I saw him get
into a cab, lean back and light a cigarette.

Murray dropped my room key on the counter between
us.

"He's kind of in a rush, I'd say." His voice was emotion-
less.

"Do you know my dad very well?" Murray was watching the cab disappear around the corner.

"Uh…he's in a lot." He turned away, busied himself at the mail slots. "You take those stairs at your right."

The stairs were steep, uncarpeted. I peered at the room numbers in the dim light. There was only a single bulb in the ceiling to light the whole hallway.

As I was making out the number on one door, it suddenly opened, and I found myself staring at a vast expanse of dirty undershirt. I slowly raised my eyes to see an unshaven, red-eyed man.

We stared at each other. He swayed slightly and I stepped back. He watched me as I found my room and inserted the key. Quickly I locked the door and pushed the bolt across.

I looked around at the brown walls, worn brown carpet—ripped near the narrow, lumpy bed—and outside the dirty window to where the flashing neon signs advertised Oyster Bar and Players Please.

I knew I couldn't possibly stay in that room all evening, especially with that creep down the hall.

I hung up my few things, put my brush, comb and lipstick on the dresser and beside them a small, nearly empty bottle of Evening in Paris cologne. Mrs. Lawson had given it to me when she was packing for Vancouver. Then I went down to the end of the hall, past the door of the man in the dirty undershirt. I could hear a radio there and a loud burst of laughter, the clink of glasses.

I found the bathroom and, after cleaning out the tub, I filled it three-quarters full. It was luxury to have all the hot water I wanted and to be able to stretch out full length. It wasn't like having a sponge bath out of a small basin the way we did at home.

I lay there, blissful, the water to my chin.

Maybe I'd meet Jack. I could wear my yellow wool dress.

Someone rattled the bathroom door handle, swore, then left. I got out of the tub, dried myself quickly, dressed and hurried back to my room. I could see by the clock in the newsstand across the street that it was nearly six-thirty. There was still time to meet Jack.

I left the hotel and turned north toward the mountains. As I walked, I wondered if Jack would be there. If he wasn't, I'd go to a movie. I passed several as I walked along Granville Street. There was one with Bette Davis that I had wanted to see for a long time, *Jezebel*.

Several people were waiting near the Birk's clock at Georgia. But I didn't see Jack until he waved at me. He'd been looking at the watches in Birk's window. Smiling, he came toward me.

"Say, this is great, Sheila! You made it!" Then, taking my hand, he tucked it into his coat pocket, and we walked to where his car was parked. It was a red Ford coupe, and he opened the door with a great flourish. "My baby," he said. "I just got it. Do you like it?"

"It's beautiful."

Jack was wearing a dark blue gabardine coat, unbuttoned, and drape pants of a lighter blue, wide at the knees, tapering at the ankle.

"You look nice," I told him, admiring the cut.

"All the guys on the boat get their drapes made in Chinatown. There's this one place…" And he told me about it as we zipped from one traffic lane to another. We had trouble finding a parking place, but when we did it was near the Bamboo Terrace. Jack said that was the best place to eat.

We ate upstairs. Jack ordered egg foo yong, chow mein and sweet and sour spareribs, and he showed me how to use chopsticks. Then he told me about being in China. He had sailed on freighters to Australia and New Zealand and Fiji. He seemed to have been everywhere.

Then we went bowling in a bowling alley off Pender. Jack showed me how to hold the ball, how to take three steps, crouching on the third, how to bring my arm back and then let the ball roll off my hand. And he was as happy as I when I made my first strike.

On our way back to my hotel, after we parked the coupe at the nearest lot, Jack and I met some other members of the crew. They were standing outside one of the hotel beer parlors.

"Jack!" they called. "Come on, buddy. Join us for a beer. We can sit on the ladies' side, eh, Sheila?"

"She'll never pass for twenty-one," said Jack. "No use trying." He put his arm around me protectively.

"Oh, I don't mind. Just as long as you don't expect me to drink beer. I've never even tasted it."

"Okay, you guys, but no horsing around." Jack pushed open the door and led us to the darkest table he could find, one in the corner. I sat farthest from the light. The waiter didn't give me a second look. He gathered up the dirty glasses and wiped the table with a cloth that my mother would have held at arm's length. Then he set down two glasses of beer before each of us.

I managed to finish one. I hated the taste, but the Chinese food had left me thirsty. Jack drank the other one for me. By the time we left at closing time, I had eaten two bags of peanuts and half of Jack's potato chips.

"What I save on beer on her, I lose on the groceries," Jack told the rest of them, but he was smiling.

Before we got to my hotel, he stopped in one of the darkened storefronts and put his arms around me.

"I had a really nice time, Jack," I said, pulling myself back. "But I'm going with somebody and he's…kind of jealous."

"No sweat," he said, dropping his hands. "Want to go out for dinner tomorrow night?"

"No, I'm going home on the seven o'clock boat. But, thanks."

"Okay, Sheila." He raised his hand in a half-salute and started off down the street, whistling as he walked.

I watched him go. I liked him very much, maybe because nothing was complicated with him.

Most of Friday afternoon was spent at the dentist. Even while sitting in the chair, my mouth numb with novocaine and the sound of the drill vibrating in my head, I relived the evening with Jack. Everything had been new and exciting—the sounds, the smells, the sights. Gibson's Landing was far away.

The nurse made up my bill. "Six fillings at two dollars a filling. That's twelve dollars." I counted out the money. It was all I'd earned in the month of Saturdays at Dr. Howard's, but it was worth it.

At Gibson's Landing there was the usual Friday night crowd to meet the boat. I didn't see Nels from where I stood on the lower deck, but I did see Jean, a girl who sat behind me at school. She left the crowd and came over to the boat.

"Sheila, guess what?"

"What?" I asked, leaning far over the rail.

Jean looked around to see who was listening, then stage-whispered, "Nels was out with Gwen Hall at Roberts Creek last night. He took her home from play rehearsal. She told everyone at school today that he kissed her." Jean had eyes that grew bigger the more she talked.

I felt as if I had been hit in the stomach.

"Oh."

"I'd sure hate to be you, Sheila." By this time Jean was standing on tiptoe, her hands clinging to the solid mesh wire that was part of the ship's railing.

"Why?"

"Arnie Olsen came back on the morning boat, and he told us he'd seen you in the Austin beer parlor, drinking beer with four guys…"

The boat's whistle blew. Jean let go of the wire mesh and stepped back on the wharf.

"I told him he was crazy," she shouted at me.

I shrugged my shoulders.

"It's okay," I said.

But it wasn't okay. I was sure of that.

11

===================

ALL DAY SATURDAY I wondered if Nels would call on me
for the dance. If he did, he'd want me ready.

After supper I dressed in my new skirt and sweater. I had
bought them in Vancouver with part of the money I'd earned
at the Lawsons'. The skirt was brown wool with box pleats,
and the yellow cardigan had small brass buttons. Nels had
given me an enamel pin shaped like a leaf and colored the
reds and browns of autumn. It was perfect with the sweater.

I put Vaseline on the ends of my eyelashes. My hair had
grown out of the feather-cut. Nels said he liked long hair,
and already it was down to my shoulders.

Four or five times I thought I heard Nels' truck, but I
was always disappointed.

My mother, who was polishing the cook stove with a

crumpled newspaper, was still questioning me about Dad and Vancouver. She'd been asking the same things since I got home.

"Tell me, Sheila," she said, as if it had just occurred to her. "Did your father say what he was doing that he couldn't even take you out for dinner?"

"No, Mom. I already told you everything." Which wasn't quite true. I'd left out the part about him being all dressed up, nervous and in a hurry.

"Do you think," she said, trying to sound offhand, "that he has another woman?"

"Mom, I don't know!"

But my mother wouldn't let it drop. She worried away, returning to it again and again. It was the same way that our dog, Pep, shook an old sweater, as if it were prey.

Was that a car stopping? I looked out the window. It had begun to rain lightly and was already dark. I saw a car's headlights on the side of the road, shining through the trees.

I found my new lipstick, Tangee Medium Red, and put it on carefully. There were only a few drops of Evening in Paris left. I pressed them on my temples, in the hollow of my throat.

"Do you know where my jacket is, Mom?" I rushed around. "Nels and I are going to the dance. I'll be home about twelve." I paused at the back door. "Mom, maybe Dad had some business of some kind. Something to do with that job he wants in the interior."

"I doubt it. Unless it was monkey business." She rattled

the grate of the stove, pulled out the drawer of ashes rough-
ly. But I was already halfway out the door.

When I got to the top of the road, I was out of breath.
I made myself slow down. The truck was like a dark,
crouched animal behind the rain-misted headlights.

Nels held the door of the truck open.

"I bet you thought I wasn't coming," he grinned.

"I didn't know," I answered. Was he making fun of me?

"Come on, don't stand there, get in." He waited until I'd
closed the door. Then, suddenly serious, he asked, "You
want to talk about it now or later?"

"Now, I guess."

We drove up the back road and pulled off to the side.
The leaves were almost gone from the trees, and bare
branches scraped at the roof of the truck. A wind gusted,
bringing squalls of rain that lashed at the windshield.

"It looks like a Squamish. Wonder if there are any dead
trees around?" I rolled down the window, stuck my head
out to look, relieved to be doing something. "None," I
reported, "but it is a Squamish."

The wind made my eyes sting. Closing the window, I sat
back again and waited tensely for Nels to begin.

He was leaning against his door, and I did the same on
my side so that we faced each other. He seemed to be in a
good mood. His mouth was relaxed, his hands loose. There
was a faint smell of whiskey in the truck.

"I took Gwen what's-her-name home on Thursday
night."

"Hall. Gwen Hall," I supplied quickly.

"Yeah, well, I guess so. And I kissed her goodnight." He waited, as if I was supposed to say something, but I didn't.

"Wanted to see what it was like, being with another girl. Maybe I was missing something." He looked at me. "Yeah, well, I wasn't…" His voice trailed off, then came strongly. "She's okay, but she isn't you."

I didn't know what to say. I felt relieved, but I wanted to stay angry with him a little longer.

"There's no use pretending you're so innocent, Sheila. Arnie Olsen came back from Vancouver, and he couldn't wait to tell me about you and the guys from the boat."

"But I didn't kiss anyone."

"No, I didn't think you would. You've got to admit, though, Sheila, it didn't look good."

"I know that," I said. "I'm sorry, Nels. But really, there wasn't anything to it!"

He leaned toward me.

"Don't do it again," he said, taking hold of my hand. "Okay?"

I pulled my hand away and faced the front of the truck. The wind was whining through the cracks.

"How about you? Doesn't it work both ways?"

"I told you before, Sheila, not to be too sure of me."

"Sounds kind of one-sided." My hands were tight fists at my sides.

"Sure it's one-sided. What's the matter with that?" He grabbed my hand again, this time pinning it down so that

I couldn't pull it away. "You know you can't stay mad at me," he said, laughing now as I tried to yank my hand from under his. "Let's forget it, okay? Come here, I haven't kissed you for—how many days? Too many, anyway."

He began to unbutton my sweater, then bent suddenly to kiss the top of my breasts. He had never done this before, and I felt a swift, sweet stab in my lower stomach.

I could see the shape of his head, how it curved. And the long line of his neck. It made me ache.

He brought his head up then and kissed me, his mouth opening slightly on mine until finally he pulled back and said, his voice unsteady, "If we're going to the dance, we'd better go."

Was this the way he had kissed Gwen, I wondered?

He switched on the headlights. The rain was sheeting down; it was almost like being under water. The wind slapped wetly at the windows.

By the time we got to the dance, the rain had slackened, but the wind was stronger than ever. It was a strong Squamish. It had funneled down between the mountains at the head of the Sound and would finally blow itself out past the Gap. Now it whipped at us as we ran from the truck to the hall.

I loved dancing with Nels; he was easy to follow. And it was wonderful to be with him again. No one cut in on us. It just wasn't done, not for a couple going together as we were. Nor did Nels dance with anyone else.

The only times he left me were when he went out-

side to have a drink with his friends. He went out four
or five times in the evening. Each time he stayed a little
longer.

Embarrassed to be standing alone waiting for him, I
went into the girls' dressing room. It was where we changed
for basketball, and there was always a strong smell of running shoes and stale gym clothes. The room had a few
hooks on the wall, a cracked and wavy mirror, a bench on
either side. It was empty now as I combed my hair, trying
to find a place on the mirror that didn't divide my head in
two.

Then I saw the blur of another face in the mirror. It was
Gwen Hall. She took a step backwards when she saw me,
then changed her mind and came in.

"Hi, Gwen," I said.

She seemed relieved, friendly. She flipped up her skirt
and yanked down her blouse and then began to comb her
hair, which was blonde and naturally curly. Her large
brown eyes stared at me. She always reminded me of a yellow pansy with a velvet brown center.

"I hope you're not mad at me," she said, getting out her
lipstick, a poppy pink. "About Nels." She put the lipstick
on carefully, running the top of her little finger lightly
around the outline of her lips. She worked her mouth. "I
didn't go after him or anything. I knew you were going
with him."

"That's all right." I found it easy to be friendly. I was the
one Nels loved. "Don't worry about it."

"He is nice! Though all he did was talk about you." She turned to me. "Sheila, you're so lucky…"

"I know," I answered, feeling privileged. Everyone liked Nels.

We left the dressing room together. Arnie Olsen was waiting for me just outside.

"You'd better come," he told me. "Nels is sick."

"Sick? Where is he?" Worried, I followed him down the short hall.

"Out back, in his truck. He wants you."

We had trouble pushing open the door against the wind. An empty garbage can rattled across the back porch. The rain had stopped, but the ruts and holes in the parking lot were filled with water, and it was impossible to avoid stepping in them. Arnie came as far as the truck, then left me, hurrying back to the hall.

Nels was sitting on the passenger side of the truck, hunched over.

I put my hand on his shoulder.

"What is it, Nels? Do you hurt somewhere?"

He didn't seem to hear me. The truck reeked of whiskey. I rolled down the window, but the wind filled the truck. Hurriedly I closed the window except for a crack.

"What's the matter? Arnie said you were sick. Do you feel like throwing up?"

He groaned and turned away from me. I didn't know what to do. Nels' face was wet with perspiration, and he breathed in short, panting gasps.

"Nels, I'm going to get one of the boys to take you home."

He didn't answer, but turned back, putting his head down on my shoulder. I put my arms around him.

After a minute, I felt him stir, become restless. Then he lunged to open his door. I could hear him retching out on the grass.

He was still vomiting when I left to find Arnie.

Arnie was hanging around the back door. He seemed surprised to see me.

"I thought you were with Nels!"

"I was. I don't know what's the matter with him, other than he's had too much to drink. Would you take him home?"

"Oh, yeah, sure, Sheila. Sure thing. I'll get a couple of the guys."

I found my jacket under the pile of coats at the door and hurried back outside. I watched Arnie and Doug Jackson support Nels between them as they walked him to Doug's car. I saw Nels bend over, being sick again, before he got in.

When they drove off, with Arnie and Doug in the front, Nels had his head hanging out the back window.

I had a four-mile walk home. I bent my head into the wind and pulled my jacket collar up as far as it would go. By the time I was through Gibson's Landing, I was soaked, my feet sloshing in my shoes and my new skirt, heavy and wet, dragging with every step I took. Going through the Indian reserve where the trees grew right to the edge of the road, I heard ominous creaks and groans. Branches were blowing off trees and into the road. Once in a while a tree splintered with a shriek and crashed.

I began to run, not knowing if I was running away from a falling tree or into one.

It was black. Black sky, black forest. Only my feet felt where the surface of the road was. Waves were pounding on the beach below me. The wind was a banshee—eerie sounds, screeches, sighs, groans, cries, moans.

Down hills, around bends, along level stretches. I'd never get home. There wasn't a car on the road, but I began to feel the presence of somebody—something—near me.

So strong was the feeling that I stopped to listen. The high-pitched wail of the wind, the splitting groans of trees, the surf crashing on rocks. My heart pounding loudly in my ears, and a sound of heavy breathing.

I took one step forward and walked into a large, hot, breathing body—hairy, moving. I sank to my knees, waiting for the blow.

Only a cow. There was a faint jingling of a bell, a loud moo as she moved away. A swish of her tail caught the corner of my eye.

I moved through the herd, bumping into sloping flanks, slipping in cow patties and crying with relief.

Two hours after I had left the hall, I pushed open the kitchen door of our new house. The recently acquired electric light was too bright for my eyes after the black night.

My mother, who had been writing a letter when I burst in, took one look at me and said, "Glory be to God! Whatever has happened to you?" She helped me off with my wet jacket and, scolding and comforting, she had me sit in front of the kitchen stove and opened the oven door for more warmth. "You've walked all this way home?"

I wrenched off my sopping shoes and flung them on the open oven door.

"I have," I burst out. "It isn't fair! Girls have to be so… nice! We can't do or say anything! But we're supposed to put up with anything anyone else does. I hate being a girl!"

"Now, Sheila, calm down. It'll be all right." She filled a basin with hot water, handed me the soap. While I washed, she hung my nightclothes over the stove to warm, something she did only when we were sick. "The men don't have such an easy time of it, either."

"Name me one thing! Just one!"

"Two. I can name you two. Come on, sit down, I've poured you a cup of tea. There's not many things a cup of tea won't help."

I sat across from her, wrapping my wet hair in a towel.

"For one thing," my mother continued, "they have to worry about work, making a living for us."

I stared at her. Had she forgotten Dad?

"And for another thing." Her voice lowered. "They have a stronger drive than we do." I knew she meant sex. "It can be dreadful hard on them."

"I still don't think it's fair!"

"Nobody said it was going to be fair." My mother's voice was mild. "It never has been, as far back as time. For anybody."

12

================

NELS PROMISED not to drink again if I promised not to meet the Union steamship. I told him I wouldn't if it meant that much to him.

I missed going, though. There was so little to do at the Landing that the steamship calling in was the highlight of the day. And I liked walking up the wharf with Mr. Percy after the boat had pulled out. He always had some news. Had he told me that Helga was talking more these days? And that Dr. Howard had mentioned to him that I was "a right smart girl and pleasant to boot"? And so he went on, sure that in me he had a captive audience.

Of course, I'd miss Jack, too. Whenever I saw him he reminded me of the excitement, the things to do in Vancouver. There were times I felt pressed between the mountains at the back of me and the ocean in the front, and I thought I couldn't wait to finish school and leave the Landing.

But I still loved school. My brother Tom and I were taking Science 12 together even though he was a grade behind me. That's the way it was in our small high school with only the one teacher. We had to double up on some courses. Sometimes Tom got a higher mark, but that only made me study harder to beat him the next time.

My father had decided to leave Jericho Airforce Base and go to Williams Lake to work at the placer gold mine. My mother was unhappy about this. But he said he'd send sixty dollars every month.

My mother was even talking about buying a piano secondhand. Mrs. Robinson on the North Road had tacked a notice on the bulletin board at the post office: *For sale, cheap, piano in A-1 condition. B. Robinson, North Road.*

"Of course," sniffed my mother when she read it, "that means the piano would have to be washed down with Lysol before I would let it in the house. They say she has a social disease."

"You mean like T.B.?"

"No, I mean syphilis. She's been a loose woman."

* * *

"Agnes," said my father, home for the weekend, "how would you like that piano for a Christmas present?"

"We can't afford it," my mother said. "Don't be daft."

But we could see that she was excited by the idea. She went through her music sheets, which were stored in the cedar chest.

"Do you remember this?" she asked my father, and she began to hum "The Flower Song," following the notes with her finger. She could read music. My father played by ear.

Dad went ahead anyway and bought the piano, even though Christmas was two months away. He had it delivered when my mother was out at a Water Board meeting. I wiped it with a cloth wrung out in a hot water-and-Lysol solution, then dried it and rubbed lemon oil into the wood grain. It was made of cherry wood, and when I had finished, it glowed with a soft red sheen. The ivory keys were faintly yellowed, but the tone was good. Dad said he'd have a man come out from Vancouver to tune it.

Helga had shown me how to embroider, and I had already made a dresser scarf with yellow butterflies and bluebells for Mom's Christmas present. I smoothed it out on the piano and placed the picture of Grandma Brary in the middle.

"Oh, you shouldn't have, Frank!" my mother said when she came into the living room at Dad's urging. "You really shouldn't have."

She walked, trancelike, over to the piano, sat down at the bench and began to play. Her fingers, stiff and unaccustomed to the keyboard, still remembered how. And she was still playing hours later when I went to bed.

* * *

One evening, Nels' parents invited me to dinner. I just dreaded the thought. I wanted to like Nels' mother. Why should I care if she wanted to look like a teenager?

I didn't taste anything because I was trying so hard to make a good impression. But I probably didn't. Mrs. Bergstrom asked me how school was going, and I told her about studying *Macbeth*.

"Mac who?" she asked.

"You know—Shakespeare."

"Oh, him." There was a silence. "Nels, pass Sheila the ketchup."

Later when Mr. and Mrs. Bergstrom left for the Legion to drink beer, I did the dishes. Nels sat and read at the kitchen table to keep me company. He hadn't been kidding when he'd told me he liked comic books and Westerns. He actually had a pulp Western propped up against the salt and pepper shakers as he read about the adventures of Luke, Montana Ranch Hand.

Still, at the end of the evening I felt uncomfortable— about Shakespeare and about Nels reading pulps.

The next day Nels told me, "My mother thinks you're pretty. She isn't too happy about you being a Dogan, though."

"Dogan?"

"Yeah, you know, Catholic. Says you'll want to get married and have a kid every year."

"I'm not getting married for a long time, Nels Bergstrom, so you don't need to worry about that!"

We were sitting in his truck after school. It had begun to snow lightly, the flakes melting as soon as they hit the window.

Nels took my hand and turned it over, tracing the lines on the palm.

"How long before you want to get married, Sheila?"

"Well, I want to finish high school first, then go on to university or nursing school, then I want to work for a few years, travel…"

"What am I supposed to be doing all this time?" Nels asked.

"I don't know. What do you want to do?"

He watched the snow coming down, heavier now. It blanketed the windows and shut us in a small, silent white world.

"I want to get married. Build my own house. Have a kid or two." He turned on the engine. "You cold?" He pulled me closer, wrapped his arms around me and blew down my neck.

"I'd like to get married, too, Nels, but not for a while."

"Sheila, I mean soon. What do you think it's like for me, having to leave you every night, go home and…"

"Go home and what?" He had completely unbuttoned my blouse by then—the snow was giving us privacy—and was stroking the skin of my breasts very gently with his fingertips. At times he was so tender that I thought I would melt. Other times he could be crude and rough, and I would pull back, afraid.

"And what, Nels?" I asked, not really wanting to know, only wanting to prolong what he was doing.

"Take care of myself..."

"What do you mean?"

"Oh, Jesus, Sheila, don't give me that crap. Jack off, what do you think?" He took my hand then and placed it on himself.

"Undo the fly," he pleaded, kissing my ears and neck.

"No, Nels..." I started to say. Then a warmth was growing in me, spreading, like the sun rising.

He fumbled with the opening himself and took my hand. I heard him groan. Suddenly my hand was filled with a wet warmness, and Nels groped for his handkerchief and wadded it into my hand. I could hear him breathing deeply.

I dried my hand on his handkerchief and put it on the seat between us. I didn't want to look at him. His breathing slowed, relaxed,

But I didn't feel relaxed at all. My stomach felt like I'd taken a sudden lurch in an elevator, and I ached so much it hurt.

But I did know, then, what he had been talking about.

* * *

Christmas was only a month away. I sent to Woodward's for a record for Nels, Margaret Whiting's "I'm in Love with You, Honey." He always asked for it at dances.

Trust Tom to come up with the idea of a correspondence course for my mother. All the years I'd seen her read my school books, and it had never occurred to me she might like to be learning, too.

That was one of the differences between Tom and me. He was more thoughtful of the family than I was. Tom and my mother were alike that way. They were both shy and more comfortable at home.

I guess my mother was right. I was more like my dad. We both liked to be out and meeting new people. Maybe that was the reason my mother liked Tom so much and me not very much.

Anyway, Tom sent away to the Department of Education in Victoria for a catalogue, and we spent hours going through it. Finally we narrowed it down to either a poetry or a literature course.

I took my grade twelve book of poetry out to the kitchen where Mom was making plum pudding.

"Listen to this, Mom. It's by Edna St. Vincent Millay. Tell me if it doesn't remind you of Helga Ness.

"Love in the open hand, nothing but that
Ungemmed, unhidden, wishing not to hurt,
As one should bring you cowslips in a hat
Swung from the hand, or apples in her skirt"

My mother had shut her eyes when I'd begun to read. When I stopped, she took up where I left off, her eyes still closed.

"I bring you, calling out as children do:
'Look what I have!—And these are all for you.'"

She opened her eyes and, seeing my astonishment, said,
"I've always loved poetry." So Tom and I decided to give
Poetry 12 to Mom for Christmas.

* * *

Nels gave me a beautiful set of Evening in Paris for
Christmas—soap, cologne and talcum powder. I wished I
had been able to give him a nicer present.

Dad and Paul were home, and my mother cooked a
goose. We didn't usually celebrate Christmas much at
our house, but this was one of the happiest we'd ever
had together as a family. When I went to sleep, my
father was playing the piano, and my mother was
singing along.

Tom, Mike and Jim went back with Dad to spend the
holidays at Williams Lake. The house seemed empty without them.

On New Year's Eve Nels took me to the dance at
Roberts Creek, and he didn't get me home until after one
in the morning.

Mom got out of bed when I came in. With one hand
she clutched the open edges of her blue flannel kimono.

"Sheila, this is no good. This is far too late for you to be
out."

"But it's New Year's Eve! The dance didn't end until after midnight!"

"It's not that. You and Nels. You can't go on like this… or you're going to have to get married."

"What are you talking about?" I stared at her. "I don't want to get married!"

My mother drew the neck of her kimono tighter and shivered. The fire had been out for hours, and it was cold and damp in the house.

"You can't see this much of each other without getting into trouble. It's bound to happen."

I pretended I didn't know what she was talking about and went to my room. Undressing quickly, I was in bed with the covers pulled up high over my ears when she came to the bedroom door.

"From now on, you're to be home half an hour after the dance ends," she said. "No more of this wandering in late, your clothes all rumpled and your eyes bright. No more, I say. You think I don't know what's going on?"

"Yes, okay, Mom."

My mother meant business, but I didn't think Nels was going to like it.

He didn't, and he said so loudly and often. Then, two weeks later, without a word to tell me why, suddenly it was all right with him to bring me home early. And it seemed to me that he drove off quite happily.

It was Arnie Olsen who told me why. I had eaten my lunch with the other girls in the classroom and was on my way over to basketball practice when Arnie caught up with me. Both his hands were rammed down in his pockets, and his walk was cocky.

"You don't mind," his voice was casual, "Nels' trips to Gower Point?"

"You think I should?" I asked, not knowing what he was talking about.

"Well, gee, Sheila, any other girl would. I mean, even though Betty Lou doesn't charge Nels, it's still…you know what I mean."

I didn't know what he meant, and one look at my face must have told him that.

"She's that woman's moved into Smyth's old place. A chippy. Practically all the guys in town have been over there at least once. Doesn't charge much, and she's built like a brick—"

"Arnie, you can go to hell." I tried to keep my face blank, but my voice trembled with anger.

"Sorr-ree!" Arnie said and swaggered off.

When Nels took me home from the movie the next night, I asked him about Betty Lou. Pulling out his wallet, he took out a picture and handed it to me. He turned on the overhead light of the truck, and I held the color photo under it.

Betty Lou looked to be in her early twenties and was posed leaning against a car. She wore a short white dress and was laughing at something. And, in Arnie's words, she really was built.

I held the snap by one corner, as if it were dirty.

"Good looker, isn't she?" said Nels.

Dropping the snapshot in disgust on the seat between us, I said, "You really burn me up!"

"Ah, Sheila's jealous!" Nels taunted.

I raised my hand as if to slap him, but he caught my forearm and bent it backwards.

"Temper, temper, little Sheila."

I glared at him, but he just laughed. I moved to open the truck door. He pulled me back.

"What do you expect me to do?" he asked, suddenly serious. "You don't want to get married. You let me go so far and no further, and then when some dame gives it away, you want me to say no. You can't have it all your own way."

And that was the impasse. Nels took me home on time, and both he and my mother were satisfied.

I wasn't. Nels and I never talked about Betty Lou again, but I cheered when Arnie Olsen said she was moving to Alert Bay at the end of the month.

* * *

My brothers came back from Williams Lake. Only two weeks, and yet I could see that they'd grown even in that short time.

Tom was different, too. Something must have happened at Williams Lake, but when I questioned him about it, he changed the subject.

He was changing in other ways, too. He had the male

lead in the school play, and he was supposed to kiss the heroine twice.

"It's disgraceful, that's what it is," my mother told him. "Think of the example you're setting for the younger boys. Jim and Mike look up to you. Do you think the play would fall apart if your teacher changed those scenes? I've a good mind to talk to the principal about it."

Tom was stubborn and quiet.

"I'm going to do it," he said.

I saw how his hands trembled, though he hid them behind his back. My mother didn't, and she gave in.

Paul wrote that he was getting married. She wasn't Catholic, and her people were English. That was two strikes against her right there, as far as my mother was concerned.

Married. Free to do what they wanted. Nels and I were beginning to act as if we were—almost. What contortions we went through to avoid "it." Because, of course, "it" could cause pregnancy, and that must never happen. I got to the point where, if Nels had said, "Let's get married now," I would have. School seemed pale beside the urgency I felt.

Sometimes I thought it must be easier for Nels. He did have some physical relief. But I walked the trails in the woods, restless. I thought if I could walk enough, I might get rid of some of the ache. It didn't happen, and I was left wanting what I hadn't had. I didn't know what—only that I was missing it.

* * *

Dr. Howard talked to me about going into nursing.

"I'll write you a letter of recommendation that will get you into any nursing school you want. You should be taking Latin, maybe a correspondence course."

I dreaded the thought of all the extra homework that would mean.

On the other hand, I noticed that Mom didn't seem to mind the homework for her poetry course. I'd always known she was smart, but when I saw her papers come back from Victoria marked "A" in red ink, I just had to look them over.

There were scribbled comments in the margin in the same red ink: "Good work, Agnes. Keep it up," and "Shows originality," and "You could enlarge on this— most interesting."

On the last page of each paper was a section for the student's comments or questions. My mother wrote, "Thanks for pointing out poem by Gerard Manley Hopkins and for all your help and kind comments."

The next paper had this reply: "Agnes, only too glad to help someone who obviously loves and appreciates poetry as much as I do. William A. Mann."

It was strange to think of her being known as Agnes by a teacher in Victoria who thought she was an excellent student. We were all proud of my mother's marks and told her so.

"I always did well at school in Ireland," she said. "That's why it broke my heart when I wasn't allowed to go past the fourth grade. But they needed my help on the farm, and that's all there was to it."

Shouldn't she know, then, how I felt about school? Or did she feel because she hadn't had it, neither should I?

* * *

Dad hadn't written or sent any money home since Christmas, and here it was well into March. My mother was beside herself with worry. The house wasn't finished inside yet, and there were still the monthly payments to be made on the land.

Tom finally told me what had happened at Williams Lake when the boys visited Dad for the Christmas holidays.

"You should see the woman who's living with Dad. I don't know how he can stand her."

"A woman?" We were cleaning out last fall's leaves from the wooden crib that kept the milk cold and fresh in the creek. I straightened up and tucked my cold hands under my arms to warm them. "What woman?"

"He says she's his housekeeper."

"Housekeeper! I'll just bet she's his housekeeper!" I was beginning to sound like my mother.

Tom lowered the milk can back into the cleared crib.

"Yeah, well, don't say anything to Mom about it. It would only hurt her."

So we had to listen to my mother worrying about Dad

not sending her any money, and all the time we knew why.

Each day she looked for a letter from him, and there was none. She began to talk again about my quitting school.

"Either that or get married to Nels," she declared.

"I've just got a few months left, Mom!"

"May God forgive us all!" She made it sound less like a plea and more like an indictment. "To think that I should have to be back in this state, worrying about how to put food in our mouths."

Then my mother turned the bread dough onto the table surface to knead it. She sprinkled the table with flour, folding the flour sack inside out, so as not to waste one precious bit.

13

=====

MONEY FROM my father arrived sporadically. It was the uncertainty more than anything that was the hardest part for my mother.

"If I had my way," she told me, "I'd see that every woman raising a family would receive a certain sum of money every month, regardless. That way we could plan, we could save. This way we're at the mercy of the men."

My mother lost the buoyancy of the past year. Pinched lines appeared around her mouth. She pushed through each day as if it required an act of will.

Some weeks ten dollars arrived in the mail along with snapshots my father had taken of the placer gold mine and its great pipes, the raw countryside and the huge equipment used in the background. I was allowed to keep the pictures. One of the snaps was of my father sitting on a "cat." He looked completely in his element, and his open face seemed strong, ageless.

In his large handwriting he wrote about living and working in Williams Lake. I always skipped the descriptions of gold mining, looking only for personal comments. There were just a few. Usually in the last line he wrote, "My love to you and the kiddies," or "Hope Sheila is back at school and doing well, as usual," or "Tell the boys I enjoyed their visit, and I'm glad they're turning out so well," or to my mother, "Hope you are in good health and managing without too much trouble."

What my mother wrote back, I had no idea. I knew she wrote regularly and that she asked us to write, too.

* * *

"Sheila," my mother said to me one clear April Sunday when we were tidying up the kitchen after breakfast, "I'm going to put half of the land up for sale." And hanging up the dish towel, she explained as much to herself as to me, "I need to talk to Helga Ness. About the payments on the land. I don't know what else to do, I'm sure…" Her voice trailed off, then in a minute came back stronger. "Helga has a soft spot for you, Sheila. It won't hurt to have you come along."

I emptied out the dish pan, wiped it dry and hung it up on its nail above the counter. All the time I was wondering why I felt reluctant to go.

Together we walked across the bridge to Helga's place. The creek was running high with the run-off from the melted mountain snows, and I leaned over the rail to watch it swirl just inches below. I thought how sad it was that my mother had to be concerned about money again, but I felt uncomfortable that I was to be used as…almost a bargaining tool.

We found Helga outside splitting cedar kindling. When she saw us she stuck the ax in the chopping block.

"It's about the money for the land," my mother blurted out as she stood there, the crystal April sun warming our hair. And she began to tell Helga about my father working up north.

Helga listened in silence. My mother became agitated, as if the telling rekindled her anger.

"I really don't know what to do," she concluded, her voice unsteady. "Frank wrote he'd try to be home at Easter, but I don't know. I've not even enough money to feed us the rest of the month."

All this time Helga was following my mother's words closely, once in awhile giving a little nod of understanding.

My mother went on.

"And there's no sense writing his boss. I did that once years ago, and when they called him into the office about it, Frank just up and quit his job." She paused for a minute. "I could sell part of the land, I suppose…apply for welfare. I hate to do it, but I guess it's come to that. But about this month's payment for the land—"

"Is okay," Helga answered. "Pay when you can."

My mother sighed deeply, and her face relaxed. "Well, I do feel better for having talked to you." And she put out her hand to touch Helga's in appreciation.

I looked at Helga. She was smiling that special smile of hers, the one that looked like sunlight breaking on crests of waves.

* * *

Then, one day, when I came home from school, there was a young woman sitting in our living room. On the chesterfield on either side of her were scattered blue pages, pink forms and yellow cards.

My mother introduced us. She was Miss Gamon from the Welfare Department.

It seemed to me that we were all nervous and uncomfortable. Perhaps it was because Miss Gamon had to ask personal questions. Had my father a drinking problem? No, my mother answered. Had he been unfaithful? Well, yes, she admitted. My mother was embarrassed. I was furious at my father for putting us in that spot. And I hated Miss Gamon's blue gabardine suit, her long red fingernails and her smug superiority.

We did receive some money from the Welfare Department, and Miss Gamon visited us every month. Whenever she was in our house, I got out and stayed out until she had driven away in her little green car.

* * *

My father did come home for Easter. He was sitting at the kitchen table when we came in from school.

We knew he was home before we got to the house. As soon as the noise of the school bus had died down, we heard the angry voices coming up the road.

"You think you can walk in here as if nothing has happened, and we're supposed to greet you with open arms? No, Frank. Never again."

"Now, Agnes. Don't be that way. You know—"

We had to go in sometime. We couldn't stand out on the back porch all afternoon.

Tom was the one, finally, to push open the door. We all went straight to our rooms.

None of the bedrooms had doors. It was one of the details that had been left until there was more money. I heard Tom playing softly on his harmonica, and from where I sat at my desk, I could see him sitting on the braided rug in the boys' bedroom, leaning back against his bed. Jim and Mike were building a glider, and curls of soft balsa wood piled up beside them.

I pulled out my geography homework from my loose-leaf and began coloring the map of South America. Red for beef, brown for rubber, yellow for mining.

"Can you honestly expect, Frank, that I can feed the five of us on what little you send home? You can't be that daft! Some months, nothing. What am I supposed to do?

"You have the land. You can sell it," he said quietly.

My mother was crying now. "My God in heaven! The only security we have, and you want me to throw it all away."

"This owning land has gone to your head, Agnes. There's no talking to you since you got the land. You won't even let my name be on the title. What kind of wife is it who'd do a thing like that?"

"That's it. That's what's bothering you."

My father put on his logical voice.

"After all, it was my money that bought the land and built the house. By rights." And he paused as if to make his point. "Any lawyer will tell you the same thing. It should be in my name. There'll be no peace between us, Agnes, until the property is in my name."

"Your money? Your money, was it? It was the money I saved from the government allotment checks. There are wives on this peninsula who spent every cent of their allotment checks on hair perms and trips to Vancouver, and then cried poor mouth. Your money!"

"Yes, my money." My red crayon broke, dragging beef production past the borders of Argentina. "If I hadn't been in the air force in the first place, you would never have got the check. Would you?" He made it sound so plausible.

"Francis Xavier Brary! The shame of it! To twist things like that!"

"You'll never get another cent from me until that title has my name on it."

"If I thought you would act decently," my mother said in a more controlled voice, "I would put your name on it. But you won't. You never have. Why should I think you'd turn over a new leaf now? No, Frank. You can't pull the wool over my eyes again."

"Oh, for God's sake, Agnes! You're talking nonsense now. Trust a woman to get hysterical, imagining things."

There was a loud crash from the kitchen. A pot had been slammed down hard on the table.

"That's it, then," my father said. "You'll get no support from me. And don't think the Welfare Department snooping around will matter two hoots to me. I can get a job anywhere. And if you catch up with me, I'll just move on."

My mother began to shout. "The Welfare Department tells me you're living with a woman up there. If you weren't keeping her, you'd have more money to send home to your children and your wife."

"There's no sense trying to talk to you, Agnes. When you get like this there's no reasoning with you."

I wanted to go out in the kitchen and shake him. There were a few minutes of silence. I could hear my mother moving around the kitchen. The stove lid was lifted, dropped again.

Then, in a voice deadly serious, "Get out, Frank."

My heart curled in a tight ball.

"Get out right now. And don't ever come back. I'll manage somehow without you. But I'll not put up with your lies and your cheating and your women. We'd be better off if you were dead. May God forgive me for saying it. But it's true—" Her voice broke.

"If I go out that door, Agnes, I won't be back."

"Go, then! For the love of Christ, go!"

I heard the back door open. Felt the cold draft. Heard the clear barking of Pep come from a distance, the sharpness of evening in his bark.

"And you wonder why I turn to other women," my father said.

"Don't forget to take your suitcase." My mother's voice was hard. "I don't want you coming back for any reason."

The determination in her voice reminded me of her telling us, when we were younger, of how she had met our father. It had been at a dance.

"All the people I knew, they all warned me about Frank Brary. He had a bad reputation. But I wouldn't listen. I'd made up my mind. He was the one I wanted. And nothing would stop me."

Now she had made up her mind again, and with the same fierce determination. She was finished with my father.

14

"REMEMBER ALL the shooting stars last August, and how we used to wish on them?" I asked Nels.

We were down at the beach, our backs against logs, and we huddled close to each other for warmth. It was the first week in May and the evening was chilly at the water's edge.

He nodded.

"Are you sorry we left the dance early?" he asked.

"No. Especially when the fight broke out. That Arnie Olsen! Besides, it gives us more time to be alone."

"So let's not waste it. Come here."

"I am here."

"No, like this...come down here, beside me. Here, let me put my jacket under our heads."

"You're going to be cold."

"Stop talking, and let me really kiss you."

I broke away in a few minutes, but Nels was persistent. And later, when he looked at his watch and saw how late it was, I was the one who didn't want to leave.

"We've got to go," he said. "Your mother will kill you." He didn't know I was feeling almost sick with wanting him.

All the way up the trail the wanting grew. One of the large stumps at the side of the trail had hollows in it, and I stopped and leaned back into one of them. When Nels fitted his arms around me, I felt him grow hard against me. Without stopping to think, I hitched my skirt out of the way, straining to have him even closer.

"Oh, Sheila, don't do that." He seemed shocked, but his voice had thickened, and I sensed the wanting grow in him, too. I kept moving myself until I felt him fit against me. He let one hand drop, and his hand fumbled between us against the skin of my inner thigh.

"Please don't stop, Nels."

He stopped moving but stayed leaning against me. I could feel a throb where his skin touched mine.

"What can I do, Sheila?" His voice was almost a groan. "You want me to stop? I can't stop now."

"I want you inside—"

"Oh, God. Don't say that." His voice was pleading, although he held me even tighter.

But I had already freed one hand and pushed the elastic down and out of the way until I felt the rayon in a heap around my ankles. I stepped clear.

I heard Nels' sudden intake of breath, and then I felt a quick hurting that seemed to tear me. My knees gave way so that I partially collapsed. But Nels held me up.

I cried out with pain. But he didn't stop, and then when the pain lessened, I seemed to loosen, become drowsy. Melted with pleasure, mounted up with pleasure. Stayed there, held there. A sense of danger—or excitement—held while I teetered…and fell. Such a long way down—my head would crack when I hit. Instead I came down into soft deep water that folded over me, rocked me.

I opened my eyes. The trees were black lace against the sky. A full moon lighted up the woods, Nels' face. His eyes were closed, his face peaceful.

After that we forgot about time. I felt the springiness of moss under me and the pressure of twigs digging into my back. Once I noticed the shape of alder leaves, black against the moon.

But always there was Nels. The smell of his hair was grass drying in the summer sun. His hands were pale flowers, his back a long line over me. And his mouth was open and loving and tasted like petals.

All around us the woods were quiet. The night itself was a soft, dark country.

It was late—too late—when we finally checked the time. But, dazed and uncaring, we wandered up the trail.

The house was dark. My mother usually left the light on in the kitchen window. Quietly, I let myself in the kitchen door, and without stopping to wash or brush my teeth, I tiptoed in the dark to my bedroom, undressed quickly and got into bed.

I was floating off to sleep, still feeling Nels' presence, when I heard my mother get up. The light went on in the kitchen. The sounds she made were purposeful and deliberate. I heard her open the back door and go out.

She was gone for over three hours.

I slept in short snatches, tight with tension. The window in my room was beginning to show light behind the thin white curtains when I heard the back door open again. Her footsteps, now tired, dragged across the kitchen, turned into her bedroom.

I heard her sit on the bed. Its protesting springs sounded short and distempered. Her shoes dropped to the floor, were pushed aside. I thought I heard a long sigh as she lay down. Birds were beginning to sing in the early morning light. They went wild when the sky turned rosy.

I found I could hardly breathe, and my mouth was dry. I dreaded the moment when I had to get up and face her. My heart was beating inside my chest, as out of control as the birds in the woods outside my window.

15

"A FINE THING," my mother said. "Traipsing in at two o'clock in the morning." She was watching me while I filled my bowl with Sonny Boy cereal, her eyes glinting with anger.

"You think I raised you to be some sort of a tramp? A slut at sixteen?"

I couldn't answer. The early morning sunlight was shining in across the kitchen table. Last night seemed unreal. It didn't belong with the bowl of brown sugar, the rainbow that was refracted from the cut-glass salt and pepper shakers, or the clean housedress my mother wore.

"What have you to say for yourself?" But she didn't wait for an answer. "When I told the Bergstroms last night—or should I say, early this morning—that I would have no more of it, they had to agree. You and Nels are to stop seeing each other. Or get married. One or the other."

So that's where she'd gone—to Nels' house. He would hate that. And so would Mrs. Bergstrom.

My mother's voice went on and on. The words banged in my ears. My head hurt. I tried once or twice to answer her, but she didn't stop talking long enough to listen. I kept trying to swallow my porridge, but it seemed to stick in my throat.

I had never seen her in such a state. It was as if everything she had held back since that final fight with my father came pouring out at me. It was a flood of anger, bitterness and frustration, and I felt swamped by it.

I had to talk to Nels, to decide what we should do.

Nels didn't call for me after school on Monday. On Tuesday I waited for half an hour after the school bus left, hoping he would come. Wednesday and Thursday I walked home, wanting each truck to be his. By Friday I knew something was terribly wrong.

I was halfway home on Friday when Nels' truck did come along the road and parked a few yards ahead of me. I ran to catch up to it. I was almost crying with relief to see him at last.

It wasn't Nels. It was Walter Bergstrom, his stepfather, who opened the truck door to greet me.

I turned away. I didn't want to talk to him. But then, maybe he had a message from Nels.

He got out of the truck slowly, and we stood looking at each other.

"Where's Nels?" I asked, my voice unsteady.

"Come on and sit down," he said, and we sat on the bank at the side of the road. The drainage ditch in front of us sparkled in the sunlight. I could see the speckled gray and white mountain stones that lay beneath its surface.

"You know," he began, "when your mother came to the house—" He hesitated. "You mustn't blame her for what happened. She's got an awful load for any woman to carry. She's worried. Naturally."

"What exactly did happen?" I had trouble getting my breath.

"She hasn't told you?"

"No." Oh, God, don't let it be too bad. I knew what my mother was like when she was angry. She was capable of saying anything.

"Are you sure you want me to tell you?"

"I was hoping Nels would."

"You haven't seen him, then, at all?"

"No. I thought maybe he'd been busy. We're supposed to go to the movies tonight. I'll see him then."

"Oh, Lord," he said. "It's just too bad."

Mr. Bergstrom patted my shoulder awkwardly and handed me a none-too-clean handkerchief for the tears I couldn't hold back.

"Your mother made it pretty clear that…I don't think Nels wants to stand in the way of your finishing school."

"She made what clear?"

"That that's what you wanted to do."

"What did she say exactly?" Yes, if it suited her, she would say that about school.

"That you were to finish school. And she said Nels is not to see you again."

"She said what?"

"Nels is not to see you again. She really caused a storm at our place. She was…uh…pretty mad, all right. Said some unforgivable things to Nels. To my wife. And for over an hour she acted almost…crazy, in a way. I hate to say that."

"Oh," I managed. I hurt in a way I had never hurt before.

He went on. "Actually, we had a pretty hard time quieting her down, getting her to leave." Oh, Nels.

It was all over. All around me were signs of summer coming—lush green, squirrels racing along the moss-covered logs, the water in the Sound showing blue and calm. A hawk circled overhead, and crows rose in a black cloud, protesting.

"Would you tell Nels I have to talk to him?"

"I'll tell him. Just don't get your hopes up. He can be pretty stubborn. Pretty girl like you—you can have your pick. Don't waste your time being unhappy about this. Finish school. And try not to hold this against your mother."

The words, spoken aloud, made it final. It was all over.

I heard the truck long after it disappeared around the bend of the road.

I wasn't surprised, when I got home, that my mother continued to ignore me. She looked up from the stove where she was browning meat for a stew and then stared back down again at the pan. Neither of us spoke. We had hardly spoken to each other all week.

I put away my books and began to set the table for supper. We were enemies, my mother and I, and the kitchen was startled and sharpened by our hostility. The knives glittered on the table. The shining steel of the warming closet over the stove reflected and distorted my mother's face, turning it into a leer. In the stove, the wood spat and hissed. The meat seared, smoked blue.

At supper I pushed the meat around my plate, drank a little milk and was glad when the meal was over. I couldn't bear the sight of everyone opening their mouths and filling them with food—chewing, swallowing.

After the dishes were done I decided that if Nels didn't come, I'd go to the movies on my own. I could sit with the girls from school.

I dressed carefully, choosing a soft blue sweater that Nels liked. Seven o'clock. Seven-thirty. My mother was watching out of the corner of her eye. Seven-thirty-five. My knees were trembling. Seven-forty-five. It was too late for me to walk to the movies in time to see the beginning of the feature. I waited until eight, then left anyway. My mother's face burned accusingly before me as I went up our trail.

Nels wasn't at the movies. I slipped in beside Jean from school. Her big eyes turned to me.

"Why aren't you with Nels?" she asked in a loud whisper.

The girls in the row in front of us turned around in disapproval.

"Shhh," said one.

On the screen, Edward G. Robinson was wounded and dying. I sat on the folding chair in the darkened community hall at Gibson's Landing and knew exactly how he felt.

The movie seemed to go on and on, none of it making any sense. When the projector broke later, I used that as an excuse to leave, then ran down the school hill to Nels' house.

Rocks rolled under my feet. Once I fell. The air was cool on my burning skin. I only wanted to be near Nels.

At the Bergstroms' the lights were on in the living room and kitchen. I sat down on the steps of the post office across from the house and watched.

His truck was there, parked along the side of the house. I saw a movement in the kitchen.

It was Nels. I saw him take a cup to the stove, pour from a pot, sit at the table before the window.

Could he see me? I moved farther back into the shadows. It looked as if he were reading.

I sat there until I went numb. The lights were finally turned off, except on the sun porch where Nels slept. Then that light, too, went out. The house was dark.

I pictured him lying in bed, his arms under his head, his long legs stretched out, the sheets rising a little, over him, there.

It was over. He didn't love me. How could he not love me?

16

═══════

A LETTER from the law firm of Starr, Nicols and Swan came addressed to my mother.

> Dear Madam:
> This is to inform you that your husband, Francis Xavier Brary, of Room 202, King George Hotel, Granville Street, Vancouver, B.C., has instructed us to proceed against you in the matter of his lawful rights pertaining to the property and dwelling of Lots 9 and 10...
> Yours very truly,
> E.B. Starr

"He wants it for that woman," my mother declared. "Well, over my dead body."

She brooded over the lawyer's letter. Finally she got in touch with Miss Gamon at the Welfare Office.

"To think," she said to us after she'd made the phone call from Mr. Percy's, "that he would do such a thing. That's what's galling. And after all I've done for that man. Scrimped and saved. Done without."

She went on all that evening until we went to bed. How poorly he had treated her, the shame of it all, how he would be punished—if not in this world, then in the next.

The next day was more of the same, only by now my brothers were getting tired of it. The same grievances were gone over again and again, almost as if she were saying her rosary. The women he'd had, the poverty, the cruelty.

Jim was the first to tire of it and leave. Then I saw Mike slip out the back door, followed soon after by Tom.

I was in my room reviewing my science notes when my mother came to the door. I looked up from my books.

"And you're just like him." Her voice lashed out at me without warning. "Look at you!"

My mother was working herself into one of her rages, when she could say or do anything. Her rages had always frightened me, and I knew that whatever I said or did would only make it worse.

"Selfish," she went on. By now she was shouting. "The very same make-up, the two of you. And," she paused—but only, it seemed to me, for effect— "moping around because of Nels. The long face on you. Now you know what it's like." A note of what sounded like triumph in her voice. "It hurts, doesn't it?"

She always went on like this. I had to let her vent it all on me. But this time it seemed endless.

"You always get what you want." She spoke as if she hated me. "Don't you? In spite of everything. Oh, the selfishness of you both!"

I went to sleep that night with her words chasing each other in my mind and woke with a headache. She started in on me as soon as I appeared in the kitchen for breakfast.

"Why weren't you up helping me? I suppose you think you're too good for that." She was still shouting at me when I ran to catch the school bus. Her words followed me up the trail. "Haven't I worked and slaved for this home?" And then, just before I reached the road, the refrain, "Why do you get what you want, and I don't?"

My stomach churned. I felt sick. But although I knelt and gagged at the side of the road, nothing came up.

All morning I was ill. No one spoke to me. I was on the outside at school now, too. I was no longer Nels' girl.

I was in the cloakroom, putting away my sweater and lunch bag, when Arnie Olsen came pushing in behind me. He stared at me—there—his eyes mocking.

Lolling against the wall, he said in a lazy drawl, "You giving away tail, Sheila?" I could hardly believe he'd said it. "Can I have a piece?"

I stared at him until his eyes finally dropped, and he turned away.

All the rest of that day I kept hearing the way he had snickered.

Did everyone know? Did every whisper or look in my direction have to do with what had happened between Nels and me?

I couldn't bear to think that Nels had told, even though I knew that boys did tell each other. Somehow I thought that loving Nels and having him love me would make it different for us.

I couldn't keep my mind on what the teachers were saying and my head ached all the time.

But it was the rage my mother directed toward me each day that was the hardest to bear. It was as if I was being pounded by her words, and it got so bad that I couldn't think, couldn't do anything except wish desperately that she would stop.

The school principal stopped me one morning in the hall.

"Is there anything, Sheila…any way at all I can help you?"

"No," I answered, unable to say more. How could I tell him I was afraid my mother was crazy and that I was going crazy, too?

Then one day I came home from school to find that a letter had come from Miss Gamon. In a neat, cramped script she wrote that there was nothing to worry about, that my father had no claims on the property. She wrote that my mother was to ignore the lawyer's letter and, above all, not to sign anything.

My mother was working among the strawberry plants. I could see her through the kitchen window. Gone were the rigid, high shoulders, the thrust-forward head. Instead she moved in a quiet, relaxed way.

And when she came into the house, a small bowl of ripe berries in her hand, she offered me some.

My mother was back to normal.

But as the days passed, I had a new worry. The nausea continued.

"Oh, God," I thought, panic-stricken. "Let my period be early this month. Don't let it be late. Please don't let me be pregnant."

Every time I went to the bathroom, I checked, hoping there would be a slight tinge of pink. Whenever I had a heavy, dragging sensation in my stomach, I had a great sense of relief. It was going to be all right. I was going to have my period after all.

But day after day passed. The time for my period came and went. Nothing happened. I was a week overdue.

Pregnant. In the morning it was the first thing I thought of. At night it was the last thought before I went to sleep. Once I even dreamed about it. The thing inside me was growing, growing bigger, and I was being swallowed. Just when the moment came for me to disappear, I woke up.

This thing was already taking over my body. It was taking over my whole life. I had to do something.

* * *

The ocean was icy cold, my legs numb. They had tingled briefly when I had started the swim twenty minutes earlier, but now I couldn't feel them. There was the shape of Keats Island, its dark evergreen tips needling the sky. Behind me was the beach, deserted now at the beginning of June. The summer cottagers had yet to come.

Every day for the past two weeks I'd made myself go swimming in the cold water, hoping that it might bring on my period. That day I swam as far as I could, my heart aching in my chest, my wind gone.

It would have been so easy to become exhausted, to let myself go. To sink below the surface. Yet even as my mind pictured this, my body refused to let it happen. I found myself floating on my back. My heart gradually slowed its rapid tripping. I gulped great, belly-deep breaths of air.

The sky above me was a pure blue, the cirrus clouds virgin white. Gulls with spotless snow breasts flew over me; even the gray of their backs seemed innocent. Their cries were the only sounds I heard. The water rocked and soothed.

It seemed to take hours to swim back. There were times when I was sure I wouldn't make it. My heart hurt. Often I stopped and floated on my back until the pain lessened. When I finally reached the shore of our beach, I crawled out of the water and lay, completely spent, a few feet above the water line.

* * *

I wrote Nels a note asking him to meet me and slipped it under his front door one evening when it was dark. But he didn't reply.

I was more resigned now. I made myself concentrate on finishing off school and the coming exams. Every day the pregnancy was becoming more of a fact, even though I'd tried everything I'd ever heard of to end it, even horseback riding.

Our graduation party was held in the community hall, which was decorated with pink and white crepe paper streamers. The basketball nets held pink and white balloons, and more balloons were stuck at random on the walls.

I wore my loosest-fitting dress—a white shirtwaist that Nels particularly liked—and I felt damp with sadness when I put it on. It was too snug at the top. I had to leave two buttons undone.

The principal gave a speech about a part of our life being over. All the girls cried, and some of the boys laughed nervously. Arnie Olsen, in a gray suit and a tie—blue with red dots, like currants scattered on it—looked almost handsome.

Nels wasn't there, of course. Jean told me he was taking out Emma Hoffman, a skinny redhead who worked at the telephone office.

As soon as the speeches were over and the diplomas had been handed out, Jean and I headed for the dressing room to comb our hair.

"Jean," I said, trying to sound casual, "is anyone having a party after the dance?"

"Gee, Sheila, I don't know. But I'll ask around. You want to go?"

"Mmmm," I said around bobby pins. "Is there any chance I could stay overnight at your place?"

"Sure. That's okay by me, but what's your mother going to say?"

"Tom can tell her where I am."

I'd heard somewhere that women who wanted to miscarry took castor oil and drank a lot of gin. The castor oil—two ounces of it—was in a bag in my jacket pocket. All I needed now was the gin.

But later at the beach party down at Gower Point, no gin was being passed around. Beer, rye, a few bottles of wine, but no gin.

"Gin?" Arnie asked. "Whatta you want gin for?" He'd taken off his tie, and it dangled from his pocket like a blue snake with the measles. "It's a sissy's drink."

"It's a lady's drink," I told him. "Come on, Arnie. Be a sport and get me some."

"You sure you wouldn't like a beer? I thought you liked beer."

"I'm sure, Arnie. I know you. If anybody can get it, you can."

Half an hour later, Arnie appeared with a brown paper bag in one hand, the neck of a gin bottle sticking out the top.

"It can't be very good stuff," he said, breaking the seal. "It only cost three bucks. But it's all I could lay my hands on."

Arnie sat on the sand beside me, poured the gin into a paper cup and passed it over to me.

Was I supposed to take the castor oil before or after the gin?

It would have to be after, when no one was looking.

The taste of the gin and 7-Up was too sweet, but I made myself drink it. Before I'd finished, my face started to tingle. Then it went numb. Arnie stared at me.

"Jesus, Sheila! What are you trying to do? Get pissed? You're supposed to make it last."

Between frozen lips, I tried to explain to Arnie that I wanted another drink. I held out the paper cup.

"Oh, no," said Arnie, backing away and hugging the bottle to his chest. "You've had enough."

It took nearly an hour to talk Arnie into giving me another drink. After, he and Jean pulled me over to the beach fire and made me eat a hot dog and then a toasted marshmallow. I barely had time to make it away from the fire before it all came up, and I was left smelling sour and with tears rising up in my eyes.

Jean and I left soon after, but before we got into her house, I threw up once more in her mother's geraniums. I think I passed out on the spare cot in Jean's room.

I woke with the sun shattering my eyeballs and my head feeling as though it were made of broken egg shells. Wandering through the house, looking for the bathroom, I discovered that no one was home but me. Everyone else was up and out.

Then I noticed the time. Ten o'clock! I should have been at work at Doc Howard's at nine. I scribbled a note of thanks to Jean and left it on her pillow.

As I hurried along the road, I thought about what to do. All month I had concentrated on studying for exams and finishing grade twelve, trying to push everything else from my mind. Now that it was over, I had to take the next step, whatever that was.

I would go into Vancouver and find a job. And then… I would decide what to do about being two months pregnant.

I heard a truck come round the bend of the road. It slowed down. I turned to look, the dust settling. Suddenly it changed gears, revved its engine and sped away, throwing gravel.

But I had time to see Nels' face. In that moment I caught a glimpse of his expression—jaw set, eyes straight ahead.

He looked as though he hated me.

17

HELP WANTED FEMALE.

I spread out the classified section of the Vancouver *Sun* on the café counter and pushed my coffee cup away.

Typist, some bookkeeping…Lady of mature years needed in motherless home…Hostess for dining room…Want a lively, highly paid job that lets you meet interesting people from all walks of life?

That one sounded too good to be true. But another one looked promising. Jolly Jumbo Drive-In. Waitresses and kitchen help wanted, top wages and working conditions, afternoon shift, uniforms and meals provided.

I circled it with my pencil. The address was in the south end of the city but on the streetcar line. It would be easy for me to find.

I had come into the city on the early morning boat, my belongings packed in a small cardboard box and with twenty-seven dollars in my purse. I had the feeling I was stealing away in the dawn. Only Mr. Percy was up that early, to take the head line of the *Lady Alexander* when she docked just before six. The sun had been up long enough to take the chill off the air, but the morning still had a brand-new feeling.

The night before I had packed and set the alarm for five o'clock. No one else was up when I buttered a piece of bread and drank a glass of milk for breakfast.

My mother, who was still sleeping, had left me four cheese sandwiches and an orange to take with me, and inside the lunch bag was a two-dollar bill and a note: *Good wishes go with you from your mother. Don't forget to write.*

At the top of the trail, just before I lost sight of the house, I turned. At that moment I didn't want to leave home. A movement at the window, which could have been my mother in her long white nightgown, disappeared as I watched.

After the *Lady Alexander* nosed into her berth in Vancouver, I stopped for coffee in the Union steamship's waiting room before walking up the ramp from the dock to the foot of Carrall Street. Below I saw railway tracks and the shuttling CPR trains and could smell their hot cinders mixed with the other smells of the waterfront: roasting coffee beans, coconut oil, rope, tar, diesel oil, and salt from the sea.

I felt hopeful. Anything could happen.

I went up Carrall Street to Hastings, passing old men slumped in doorways, loggers in caulk boots waiting outside hiring halls, and women—their hair tied up in kerchiefs—hurrying to the fish canneries that lay along the waterfront. The day was going to be hot. Already the sun brought out the stench of rotting refuse from trash cans and a smell of urine from corners. Its rays pierced the dusty windows of pawn shops, making halos around second-hand watches, cameras, binoculars and trumpets.

Chinese storekeepers hosed down the sidewalks in front of their shops and set displays of produce in flat boxes outside their doors. Lettuce, radishes, cucumbers and carrots made patterns of green, red and orange that brightened the shabby street.

A Number 9 streetcar clanged to a stop, and I climbed on, leaving my cardboard box up near the conductor while I found a seat where I could keep my eye on it. That and the small amount of money in my purse were all I owned.

The manager of the Jolly Jumbo Drive-In was young, brisk and efficient. He interviewed me right there on the parking lot with its smell of hot tar and car exhaust. All the while he kept his eyes on the car hops, snapping his fingers at them if they were slow to notice when a customer wanted service. The boys ran to the serving window and to the cars, balancing their trays of milkshakes, hamburgers and French fries like acrobats.

"My name's Ralph," he told me quickly. "I need a girl in

the kitchen—frying fish and chips, chicken. You can start today. Be here at four-thirty. Sign up in the office first. They'll give you a uniform. Friday and Saturday night we're open till two, otherwise you're off at one-thirty. Any questions?" I opened my mouth to speak. "Good," he said and left to check a tray that a car hop was taking to a car, sending the boy back for mustard.

"Pay's thirty-one dollars a week," he continued over his shoulder as he supervised a truck unloading at the service door. "Oh, by the way, be sure to wear something on your hair. Net, kerchief. Board of Health regulations."

"You mean I'm hired?" I managed to slip in.

"Of course. You need a place to stay?" he asked, taking in the cardboard box at my feet. "There's a Mrs. Williams rents rooms in the next block. You can't miss it, a brown house on the corner. It's the only house on the street. Tell her I sent you. Charges seven dollars a week. Likes to have people from the Jolly Jumbo." He hurried away to talk to a customer.

Mrs. Williams' house was exactly where Ralph had said. A dark-brown painted bungalow with morning glories climbing up the old-fashioned porch, it was set at the back of a narrow lot, and the whole of the area in front of the house was given over to a vegetable garden. The soil looked screened, black and moist.

Moving in and out of the raspberry canes was an older woman in a bright pink cotton dress who, when she saw me, worked her way slowly over in my direction. She stopped to inspect the size of the pea pods. She pulled a small weed, then she gathered a handful of rhubarb stalks, which she placed in her open apron.

Mrs. Williams was stocky and energetic looking, with hair that was streaked with gray. She talked all the way up the path to the front steps of the house, pointing out her prize plants. Leaving the rhubarb on the swinging wooden porch seat, she opened the screen door and led me into a cool dark hallway.

After the bright sunlight, it took a minute for my eyes to adjust. Mrs. Williams slid open stained walnut doors to show me the room for rent.

At one time it must have been the living room, because there was a small fireplace with a marble mantelpiece.

"Been renting rooms since my husband died," she explained. "He passed away seven years ago last month. Had a heart attack, he did." Her eyes magnified with tears. Absently, she dusted the top of a dresser with the corner of her apron.

"Here now, love." She was cheerful again. "See this? A lovely new mattress. Paid handsomely for it, I did, even though it was on sale." Then, pulling open the doors of the wardrobe, "There's plenty of room here for your clothes. I know how you young girls like pretty things. I did myself when I was young. But I like girls, I do. Rather rent to them than to young men. Keep their rooms clean, even if they do use more hot water. I have a boy myself. Walter, his name is," she went on and, as if summoned, Walter poked his head in between the sliding doors.

Walter looked to be close to thirty. His eyes seemed too small and looked over my head. His ears, too, were small and close to his head. A face without expression. My mother would have said he was subnormal.

"Oh, there you are, Wally," Mrs. Williams said. "Did you put out the garbage as I asked?"

Wally grinned—foolishly, it seemed to me.

"Do it now, then, there's a good lad," she said sadly, and he bobbed his head, grinned once more—this time at me—and left.

She sighed, took a handkerchief from her sleeve and wiped her nose thoroughly, first one way, then the other.

"You'll find Wally's no problem. Now and again he loses his temper. Then he's apt to shout. But pay no attention to that."

I wondered where Wally slept. Across the hall from me? I didn't know what to think. I'd heard about people like him from my mother, but there was no one at the Landing like Wally.

I followed Mrs. Williams down the hallway to the kitchen. Motioning me to sit down at the kitchen table opposite her, she told me about Wally.

"I had a kidney problem, I did." She kept her voice low. "The doctors didn't want me to get pregnant. But there you are. These things happen, don't they?" Had she guessed about me? "And in those days, dear, there wasn't much they could do about it except take me off salt and put me to bed." Did my running to the bathroom often mean I had a

kidney problem? "Not like nowadays with their new medi-
cines and machines and I don't know what else. So there it
was. And when the doctors told us Walter wasn't quite
right…almost broke my husband's heart, it did. I said to
him then, 'Mr. Williams,' I said—I always called him that,
him being so much older—'I'll not put him in an institu-
tion until I have to. After all's said and done, he's our own
flesh and blood.'

"And I've not regretted it, although, to tell you the
truth, Mr. Williams never quite accepted it. But I don't
know how much longer I can manage. He works, you
know—Wally does. He's a dishwasher at the Jolly Jumbo,
afternoon shift. Same as you."

Later I paid the seven dollars' rent in advance.

"I supply one clean sheet, pillow case, towel and face
cloth per week," said Mrs. Williams. "You're welcome to
use the laundry tubs and ironing board." And she showed
me around the house and basement.

It didn't take me long to unpack and hang my clothes in
the wardrobe. I closed its doors with a sense of satisfaction
and looked around me. For seven dollars this room was
more than I could have hoped for. There were even books
in a built-in bookcase on one side of the fireplace. I looked
through them.

One fell open to a pressed rose between its pages and a
note that read, *You know I haven't changed. It's you who has
grown distant. P.*

Mrs. Williams? To Mr. Williams?

I kicked off my loafers and lay down on the faded rose chenille bedspread. Pulling my dress tightly across my hips, I looked down and wondered if there wasn't a slight swelling there.

Which brought me back down to earth in a hurry.

Come on, Sheila, be practical. You've got a job at the neighborhood drive-in restaurant, thirty-one dollars a week. You start today. Room paid for one week. Total cash on hand, twenty dollars. And you're pregnant. You've got to do something about it. And fast. Don't think of it as a baby. It's not a baby yet. A baby's when it's born. Wally was a baby once. Never mind that. A new job. A chance at a new life.

What I wanted, I realized then, more than anything else in the world, was to talk to someone.

Mrs. Williams? No. Because of Wally, she'd never understand how I felt.

There was no one, and I felt desperate.

My father. Weren't we supposed to be alike? The last address I had for him was the King George Hotel. Somehow it seemed too much to hope for, that he would still be there. But he might have left a forwarding address.

18

Now that I had decided to try to find my father, I became impatient. I wished I'd waited a few days before getting a job so that I would have had that time to look for him.

The Jolly Jumbo was busy, hot, cheerful and noisy. I didn't have time to think about myself. I was too busy learning how to fry chips to keep up with the steady stream of orders that were shouted in through the small pass window between the grill area and the fry kitchen.

Three older women worked in the fry kitchen. They'd been there for years, they said, and their names were Bertha, Nellie and Doreen. They looked after me like three mother hens. After the supper rush was over and we were caught up on our orders, they told me to go for my own supper.

I took my plate of stew, which was the employees' dinner, outside to the lane behind the drive-in and sat on an overturned milk can. It was cooler out there, with an evening breeze that smelled of newly cut lawns.

I lifted the hair off the back of my neck. I decided to get it cut. I'd only let it grow long for Nels.

It was a relief to be out of the heat and smell of cooking oil. I started to think about my father again. I knew he'd help me—some way—if only I could find him,

"Mind if I join you?" It was Don, a university student who worked on the grill. He was the one who called in the orders from the car hops to the fry kitchen.

Without waiting for an answer, he pulled another milk can over to where I sat and began to chat. All the time he was talking to me, I wondered if he would be so friendly if he knew what a jam I was in. Then my mind began to work away again at the problem of finding my father.

"Okay?" It was Don's voice, and I'd obviously missed something.

"I'm sorry…"

"Okay if I walk you home?" he repeated. "After work?"

"Oh, sure…if you want to."

The rest of the night went quickly. Nellie showed me how to fry fish, and after she was convinced that I could do it, she sat down with her feet resting on top of the shortening pail while she had a cup of tea. And Bertha told me all about her daughter who had had innumerable miscarriages and was now walking around with a pessary inside of her.

Sometimes I thought the whole world must be pregnant. It seemed that people talked about nothing else. Or was it because my pregnancy showed, and they thought I would be interested?

Just before we went off shift, Don made me a special deluxe hamburger—mushrooms, lettuce and tomato—and a vanilla milkshake. Then he waited for me while I changed in the women's locker room.

When we got to the corner to cross the street over to Mrs. Williams' house, he took my hand and didn't let go, even when we got to her gate.

"You're kind of quiet, Sheila. Are you tired?"

"A little." But it was more than that. My head was busy with one thought. I had to find my father. Quickly.

"See you tomorrow afternoon at work," Don said, and he pulled me gently toward him. He kissed me lightly, briefly—a butterfly kiss.

Later I stood in the shadows of the porch and watched him go down the street. He walked briskly, as if he knew exactly where he was going and why.

I wanted desperately to feel the same way.

* * *

I woke to the sound of Wally singing in a high, clear voice from the room across the hall. Sunlight bounced through the bay window and across the green carpet to where I lay in a delicious half-sleep. A faint smell of cooking oil rose from my hair.

Less than an hour later, I got off the streetcar in front of the King George Hotel. It looked the same as when I'd stayed there to see the dentist. That seemed so long ago.

Murray was still at the registration desk. I would swear he was wearing the same suit and tie. The suit was rusty brown, and the tie was broad and yellow, displaying a bare-breasted hula girl in a fluorescent green skirt.

"You probably don't remember me, Murray, but I'm Frank Brary's daughter."

I waited expectantly for him to say something, but he just went on looking at me. I dropped my eyes to the tie. The girl's stomach was too rounded. Was she pregnant, too?

I tried again. "My name's Sheila. Is my father staying here?" Murray shoved the register across the desk to me and, pulling out a small penknife attached to his key chain, started to clean his nails.

Only a few pages of the register were filled, but I couldn't find my father's name among the signatures.

"Do you have any idea where he is?"

Murray didn't bother to look up, just went on cleaning his nails.

The telephone rang, and he answered it. Two men came to the desk, leaving their keys to be pigeonholed. Murray made up a bill for someone checking out. He gave change for the pay phone. And all the while, he ignored me.

I got more and more angry. I didn't deserve this kind of treatment. Who did he think he was, anyway? Who did he think I was, to act this way toward me?

"Listen!" I said, leaning across the desk. "I don't know what's bothering you, but I want to know where my father is. And I'm not moving from here until you tell me."

I glared at the hula girl. I would have liked nothing better than to grab that tie and hang on until Murray told me what I wanted to know.

Then Murray, in a mild voice and without changing his expression—as if there had never been any lack of cooperation on his part—told me.

"He's staying at the hotel in Campbell River." And added, still in a conversational tone, "He's married again, you know."

"He couldn't be," I answered without hesitating. "He's still married to my mother."

Murray looked at me as if I wasn't too bright. I realized then that Murray would never bother to lie. Lying would be too much trouble.

At the bottom of my purse I found a dime and went across the lobby to use the pay phone. Twelve noon by the clock behind Murray's desk. Would my father be at the hotel? Out eating? At work?

My perspiring hands made the receiver slippery. Reversing the charges, I listened to the telephone operator make the connection to Vancouver Island and then Campbell River.

"And what is your name, please?"

My name wouldn't come out. I didn't want to tell her. What if she listened in to conversations? I didn't want anyone to know why I was phoning.

"What is your name?" she repeated impatiently.

"Sheila Brary." The receiver fell from my hand. I wiped one hand and then the other on my skirt.

There was a series of long rings, then I heard the hotel clerk speak.

"Yes, Frank Brary is registered here, but he isn't in at the moment. Is there any message?"

Any message. All the words seemed to be sounding down a long tunnel.

"Operator," my voice came from far away, "could you find out when Mr. Brary is expected back?"

The hotel clerk answered, "He's working out of town. All the men come in from camp late Saturday night."

"Operator," I broke in again, "could you leave a message for Mr. Brary that his daughter will phone him Sunday morning at ten o'clock?"

Breathless with relief, I leaned against the wall.

Everything would be all right now, I told myself after I hung up. Just five more days till Sunday. I could hang on for five more days.

What is your name, please? The phrase rang in my head. *What is your name, please? Your name?*

* * *

The week moved at two different paces: slow in the mornings and early afternoons when I wrote my mother or did my laundry, and fast once I got to work. There the hours seemed like minutes in comparison.

I don't know how I got up enough nerve to ask Marie, the cook, for three days off in a row—one day for one week and two days for the next. And, please, Marie, I said silently when she came to the fry kitchen with the time book tucked under one immense arm, as close after Sunday as possible. I'm counting on seeing my father.

"Monday, Tuesday and Wednesday," Marie said as she wrote my name under those days.

I couldn't believe it.

The nearest pay phone was in the Jolly Jumbo parking lot, just outside the dining room. By 9:45 Sunday morning I was there with four dollars in two neat piles of quarters and dimes beside me.

After five minutes I found I couldn't wait any longer, and I placed the call. I heard it ring through two operators, the hotel switchboard and, finally, my father's voice. It was as clear and distinct as if he were standing beside me.

A sudden welling-up of tears wet my face, filled my nose and then dripped into my mouth and ran down my neck.

"Is that you, Sheila, honey?"

I couldn't answer. I was drowning.

"Sheila, are you there?"

"Oh, Dad."

"What is it, honey? Are you all right?"

"Dad, I—" But I couldn't seem to stop crying with the relief of not being alone in this anymore.

"Are you in some sort of trouble?"

"Yes, Daddy." I couldn't remember the last time I'd called him that.

"Family trouble? That sort of trouble?" I nodded, as if he could see me.

"Okay, now, Sheila, let's take it slowly. Just start at the beginning. Where are you phoning from?"

"Vancouver. I'm working in town now."

"How far along are you?"

"About two and a half months."

"You don't want to marry the fellow?"

"No." Not that way. Only if he wanted to.

"And you don't want to have the baby?"

"No."

"If I come to Vancouver, could you meet me at, say, the King George on Granville? About noon? There's a plane out of Campbell River in the morning."

"Yes, all right. The King George on Granville at noon."

"Helen will want to come. And I want you to meet her, anyway."

"Helen?"

"My wife."

"Oh…sure."

"Snooks, don't you worry about anything. Promise me that. Everything's going to be all right, you'll see. I'll meet you then, tomorrow, twelve noon at the hotel. Goodbye, sweetheart."

And, as if moving in slow motion, I replaced the receiver, then leaned my forehead against the cool glass of the booth.

My father was going to help me. I felt as though the whole world had suddenly lightened and turned bright again.

Outside the booth, car hops hustled about, their starched white pants and shirts brilliant in the sun, coin changers jingling around their waists. Ralph leaned in the window of a jewel blue Buick with California license plates, spreading out a map in front of the driver. A large brown and black tabby cat wound itself around Ralph's legs until he absentmindedly lifted one foot and shook it loose, never missing a word as he continued to instruct the American tourist.

I decided to treat myself to breakfast in the dining room. It would take more money than I really wanted to spend, but for the first time in the past couple of months, I was hungry.

"Orange juice, pancakes and bacon, and a large glass of milk," I ordered, settling myself comfortably in the captain's chair and propping my elbows on the maple table. A small bouquet of sweetpeas sat in the center in a blue glass vase.

I didn't recognize the waitress who was writing my order, but then, she was dayshift.

"Coffee while you're waiting?" she asked, pencil hovering.

"Yes, thank you." Under the table I opened my purse. Yes, I had enough money, and even a quarter for a tip.

When I let myself in at Mrs. Williams' an hour later, feeling comfortably full, I found her up to her elbows in flour making a rhubarb pie.

"Nothing to making a light crust, I always say, if only you don't handle it too much." She flipped the pastry into a pie plate, trimmed it quickly with the side of her hand.

The kitchen was hot. I could see the red coals gleaming through the stove's draft.

"Make us a cup of tea, will you, love?" she went on, wiping the perspiration from her face.

"I've just had breakfast," I announced, "at the Jolly Jumbo dining room." I scalded the pot and added two teaspoons of Earl Grey, her favorite. "So I won't have any."

"Well, now, that's a treat! I said to myself when you came in the door, I said, 'Sheila's feeling better today and that's a fact.'"

I stood with the teapot in my hand, not knowing what to say. Did she know?

She began to cut up the rhubarb, letting the pieces fall into the pie plate where their juice stained the pastry pink.

"What do you mean, feeling better?" I asked.

"Oh, I don't know, duck. Just a manner of speaking, is all. I put it down to your not eating breakfast and all. To tell the truth, you were looking a bit peaked. I had a mind to speak to you about it. Wanted to tell you to get yourself some cornflakes from Safeway, a quart of milk, half a dozen oranges, that sort of thing. You really should eat breakfast, you know, every day. You're still growing."

I started to answer, but she raised a floury hand in protest.

"I know, I know. It's none of my business. And you want

to be saving your money. Think you can eat all you need in a day at the Jolly Jumbo. I've heard it all before. But, well, take a look at yourself. Don't you feel like a different girl now that you've a decent meal in your stomach before five o'clock?"

"You think that's all it is?"

"Of course. You can take it from Florence Williams."

Through the lattice top, rosy bits of rhubarb showed white crusts of sugar. Taking a fork, she crimped the edges of the pie and then slid the plate into the oven.

She sat down at the green oval kitchen table with a sigh, reached down and eased her shoes off, then wriggled her toes, a look of ecstasy crossing her face. I poured her tea.

The phone rang. Mrs. Williams reached up from where she sat, pulled down the receiver and listened briefly. Then she handed the phone over to me.

It was my mother. It took a minute to realize that nothing was wrong. She was worried about me, she said, and wanted to make sure I was all right.

"Mom, I'm fine!" I tried to assure her. "Honestly! I did write you another letter. I guess you won't get it until Monday. How are the boys?"

"Tom's got a good job in the mines at Trail." But she wasn't to be diverted for long. "I hope you're saying your prayers every night, Sheila. I've written Father Donnelly at Holy Rosary and told him you were living in Vancouver. I asked him to keep an eye on you. Did you go to Mass this morning?"

No, I talked to Dad this morning. But out loud I said, "No, Mom. I had to work until two this morning."

"They have several Masses on Sunday, Sheila. You could go yet today if you really wanted to."

"Yes, okay, Mom. But I have to be at work at five, you know."

"You would still have time…"

I fiddled with Mrs. Williams' teaspoon. After a brief silence, my mother went on.

"Mr. Percy sends his regards. I'm sending you a small parcel. You should get it in a few days."

Then with a few more words of caution, she said goodbye.

I went to my room and lay down.

I felt extraordinarily tired.

19

TWELVE NOON, Monday, at the King George Hotel, and there was no sign of my father. Murray worked away on a racing form at the desk, now and then looking over at me. He had given me the briefest of smiles when I had come in at eleven-thirty.

I seated myself in the worn leather armchair that faced the main entrance.

My stomach grumbled. I'd skipped breakfast again in my hurry. I had packed a change of clothing in a shopping bag and left a note for Mrs. Williams saying that I was visiting my father on my days off.

Twelve-fifteen. My bare legs stuck to the leather with perspiration. Had something happened to the plane?

Twelve-thirty. I couldn't bear it. He wasn't coming.

Grabbing the shopping bag, I almost ran out of the hotel.

Then, there he was just in front of me, getting out of a taxi. He pulled out his wallet from his back pocket and paid the driver.

"First thing we do," he said to me after he'd kissed me quickly on the cheek, "is to leave my bag at the desk. Then we'll grab a quick bite to eat."

"I thought...Helen...was coming with you," I said when he rejoined me and we were pushing through the swinging doors of the hotel coffee shop.

"Oh, she came. Wanted me to drop her off at the Bay. She's determined to do some shopping. You'll meet her later on," he added as he motioned me toward a booth at the back.

The table top was sticky. Quickly I moved my hands off the surface and put them in my lap, then put them back on the table. I suddenly didn't know what to do with them.

"Dad," I began, feeling ashamed, "I'm sorry."

"Now, never mind that, honey," he said quickly. "You're not the first one to be caught, and you won't be the last."

"I don't know what I'm going to do."

Before he could answer, the waitress came to take our order.

"Bacon and eggs, I guess," he told her. "What'll you have, Sheila?"

"The same, thanks."

"And two coffees," he added. Then he waited until she

was out of earshot before saying, "The best thing would be the capsules, and they're easiest to get hold of."

"Capsules?" What capsules? I'd never heard of them. "Will they work?"

"Oh, they'll work, all right. Brown Bombers, they're called."

"But aren't they dangerous?"

"No, not dangerous at all. Hundreds—thousands—of women have been taking them for years. Do you think you're the only one this has happened to? Sheila, girl, it goes on all the time! If every time a woman got pregnant she had the child, we'd have been crowded off the map long ago."

How did he know all these things? But, of course, I knew he would, sensed it before I had asked him to help me. Now I would know all these things, too.

Our orders arrived. Then, without any warning. "Your mother broke my heart," he told me, "when she said we were through."

I couldn't believe I'd heard him right.

"I felt so low, I thought of suicide," he went on. "Yes, Sheila. I thought the world of your mother. Would have done anything for her. But the Catholic Church..." He was silent as the waitress filled our coffee cups. "She's going to will that property to the Church. You wait and see."

He actually seemed to believe what he was saying. Did he really expect me to take him seriously? But I kept quiet. I needed his help.

"So I said to myself," he continued, wiping the egg from

his plate with a piece of toast, "that I would make myself a new life. Then I met Helen, so we got married."

"How could you marry Helen if you were already married to Mom?"

"I never married your mother," he said, as if I'd dragged it out of him. "I saw to it that you kiddies had my name on your birth certificates. I did that."

I thought he sounded self-righteous, and what he was saying seemed so absurd that I had a hard time keeping quiet.

"I'd been married before." His voice broke into my thought. "And your mother knew it."

I didn't believe him, but I asked anyway.

"Then how can you be married to Helen?"

"Divorce, Sheila."

"You can't be divorced and Catholic, Dad. Even I know that."

"I married out of the Church in the first place, and I've never gone back."

My head ached. The coffee shop suddenly seemed too hot and stuffy—stale with cigarette smoke. I wished my father would stop talking. He was confusing me.

I pushed back my plate, unable to finish eating.

"Done then, are you?" my father asked. I nodded. "Well, we might as well take a walk. The drugstore isn't far."

It was a small, crowded store, and we had to work our way slowly to the pharmacy at the back. My father spoke in low tones to the pharmacist, an elderly man, crisp in his white jacket. I wandered toward the hot water bottle display and pretended to be interested. Several times I caught the pharmacist glancing at me, and I thought his face showed distaste and even anger.

His white jacket disappeared through a door into a back room. He returned in a few minutes with a small brown parcel in one hand, put it down on the counter for my father to pick up, walked away and busied himself at the cash register, then came back and picked up the ten-dollar bill my father had left in place of the parcel.

Before leaving, my father tried to placate him. I knew the voice.

"Well, isn't it the truth, though? It happens in the best of families."

But the pharmacist turned back to his work, the expression on his face now clearly contemptuous. I felt kind of sorry for my father.

Dad placed the package in his shirt pocket, buttoned down the flap. We didn't talk much on the way back to the hotel. My father smoked one cigarette after another, and I was beginning to feel panicky now that we had the medicine. It meant that I'd be taking it soon.

Still, my father didn't seem worried. He seemed preoccupied, as if he hadn't liked the way the pharmacist had treated him. I realized then that one of my father's strongest needs was to be well thought of. Even more, to be made much of. It was the one thing my mother would not give him.

Back at the hotel, my father chatted briefly with Murray.

"Okay, Sheila," my father said, dropping a room key in my hand, "you and Helen can share a room. She'll be there if you need her. I'll be right next door."

I winced inside at the idea of being with Helen. I wished I could be by myself. I didn't think she was going to like it, either.

It wasn't until we got upstairs that my father handed the brown package over to me. It felt heavy in my hand.

"How am I supposed to take this?" I asked. It didn't sound like my voice.

"You take two capsules. Then if they don't work in four hours, you take two more. That usually does the trick. If nothing's happened in eight hours, you start all over again."

Had he told this to someone before? How many times?

We sat in the lumpy armchairs and talked, mostly about his job at Campbell River. I nodded at what I thought were appropriate times. I was scared to death, but just when I was sure I couldn't go through with it after all, the thought of having a child made taking the capsules less frightening.

While we were still sitting there talking, Helen came in. She stood in the doorway, loaded down with Bay boxes and bags. A tall woman, she had harsh features, and there was a sense of power about her.

Dumping her purchases on the bed with one abrupt movement, she sprawled in a chair, lighting a cigarette with a lighter shaped like a pistol. She blew smoke in my direction and said in a harsh voice, "So this is Sheila." Her eyes stayed on me, examined me closely.

I disliked her intensely. Her eyes darkened, and I saw in them that the feeling was mutual.

"Why don't you two girls get dressed for dinner, and we'll go somewhere really special," my father suggested. He seemed happy that we were all going to be friends.

"I can wear my new dress," Helen said, her voice light with enthusiasm now. She began to open packages, finally finding the right box.

"Do you like it, Frank?" she asked as she shook out a coral jersey dress and held it up. It showed her dark hair off to advantage, and I saw a flame flicker behind my father's gray eyes.

"Mmmmm," he said, "just beautiful." Then, "Sheila, there's still a couple of hours before dinner. Here." And he opened his wallet and pulled out a twenty-dollar bill. "Why don't you go down to the Bay and see if you can find yourself a pretty dress?"

I knew what he wanted. He wanted me to disappear for a couple of hours so he and Helen could make love.

"Sure, Dad. Thanks."

I found a summer dress—more to please my father than for any other reason—at half price because of July sales. It was made of bright yellow polished cotton with a print of small angel faces outlined in black. It was original and daring.

"We're meeting some friends from Campbell River at

the beer parlor," my father told me when we'd finished eating dinner. "You'll be all right on your own, won't you?"

I nodded, relieved that at least I could be by myself for a little while before Helen came to the room.

I checked my purse. The capsules were still there. I would be taking them soon now.

20

THE ROOM was a mess. Helen had left her clothes everywhere: a girdle tossed on the armchair, a pair of nylon stockings draped across the lampshade. Orange face powder trailed across the dresser top, and one towel hanging from the rod beside the small hand basin was smeared with lipstick, rouge and mascara.

I had to clear the bed of her day's shopping. The boxes, bags and tissue wrappings were all in a jumble. Picking up the whole lot carefully, I moved them to the coffee table.

When I had done everything I could to postpone taking the capsules—brushing my hair, washing my face, cleaning my teeth—I took the package out of my purse. I opened it.

Eight capsules. They were brown, the size and shape of cod liver oil capsules.

A small piece of paper with typewritten instructions on it was included.

Take 2 capsules and repeat in 4 hours. If necessary, repeat procedure in 8 hours. If patient becomes unconscious with weak pulse and clammy skin, seek medical aid immediately.

I let the brown capsules roll out into my palm. They were smooth, cylindrical—poisonous.

My hand trembled when I filled a glass with water, and I had to force myself to swallow one capsule, then another.

I got into bed, pulled the covers up to my chin, and waited for them to work.

But I was too tired to stay awake. Nothing was happening. I didn't feel any different. I switched off the bedside lamp.

* * *

Deep, painful cramps woke me, almost throwing me from the bed. For a moment I wasn't sure where I was. The rosy glow from the neon sign outside the window lit up the room. Then the events of the day came back to me.

There was no sign of Helen. The cramps increased. I doubled over with them. Then a wave of nausea sent me flying to the door, where I fumbled with the lock before rushing down the hall to the bathroom. I made it just in time before I was violently ill.

Perspiration sheeted my face, and my whole body trembled. My knees buckled under my weight. I sat on the edge of the cold bathtub, praying the nausea would pass. I retched again until all I brought up was green bile.

The cramping increased until I thought I couldn't bear it. Deep grinding pain. Diarrhea. But although it seemed that everything had torn loose inside me, there was no bleeding. No miscarriage.

I crept back down the hallway and into the room. Helen had come in sometime when I was in the bathroom and was lying—in her slip, her mouth open—across the bed. Her clothes lay in a tangle on the floor, and a smell of garlic and beer rose from her like a small cloud.

I eased myself into the armchair and laid my head back. The clock across the street showed three. It had been at least four hours since I'd taken the two capsules. Could I possibly take two more? Maybe now that there wasn't anything to vomit, the medicine would work.

I found my purse, took out two more capsules and filled the drinking glass at the sink. Then I let myself out of the room and eased the door shut.

Waiting until I was in the bathroom before I swallowed the capsules, I had to fold my arms tightly across my stomach and walk back and forth to will the medicine to stay down. I walked like that for about twenty minutes.

It was going to be all right. I didn't even feel sick anymore. I decided to go back to the room and try to get some sleep.

The window in the hallway near the fire escape was open, and a cool summer breeze lifted the grimy net curtains. I knelt down and rested my arms on the sill. Night sounds came from behind me: faint snores, rustlings, murmurs. And from the street below came the sound of light traffic, the beep of a horn, breaking bottles, voices raised in anger, the long drawn-out wail of a protesting cat, a siren in the distance.

I got as far as the door of the room before the second dose hit. This time it was a purge that went on and on. Only water came from my bowel. Only a blood-tinged mucus from my stomach.

Oh, let it be over! Let it stop!

Finally I lay in the tub, too weak to move and use the toilet.

When at last it was all over, I wadded my filthy nightgown into the waste basket, ran both taps and sluiced myself down as best I could. Wrapping the bathmat around me like a sarong, I dragged myself back down the hall and into the room.

Helen slept on. A bubbly little snore came from the bed. Daylight outlined the window, and the clock showed six. My tongue stuck to the roof of my mouth. My lips were cracked.

The pills were not going to work. All they had done was leave me with a raging thirst and exhausted beyond anything I'd ever imagined. And I was still pregnant.

As I dressed in the half-light, bits of the past week stuck

in my mind. Silly, unrelated things, yet they replayed themselves as if of momentous importance. That note in Mrs. Williams' book: "It is you who has grown distant...distant...distant..." "My own flesh and blood." "The best of families." "After all's said and done...done..."

I had to have something to drink. Not water—the very thought made the metallic taste in my mouth grow brassier.

Tea. That's what I wanted. I took one last look around the room to be sure I hadn't forgotten anything. With a loud groan, Helen turned over in her sleep.

The hotel coffee shop was open. Even before I got through the lobby I could hear the clatter of dishes and smell the toast and coffee. I took the first empty stool I saw and sat down with relief.

Oatmeal porridge, large bowl, 15¢, I read on the menu. When the waitress came to take my order, pencil poised over her order pad, I pointed to that item.

"And tea," I added, my dry lips sticking together painfully.

There was enough oatmeal in the bowl to feed three people. I had to eat it very slowly because my stomach felt cavernous and dark brown. After a few minutes I put down the spoon and waited, just to see how it settled.

I still felt weak and dazed and had trouble thinking clearly. There was an odd tingling sensation around my mouth and in my fingers. My skin itched all over.

I knew I had a room somewhere in Vancouver, but the harder I tried to remember where it was, the more its location escaped me.

I closed my eyes. I felt light-headed, as if I might float away.

At least the porridge was staying down. My stomach felt as tight and full as a small pup's.

This must be a dream.

Colors were vivid against my eyelids. Green woods, purple mountains, sapphire sea. And sounds echoed and re-echoed in my head. I could hear a robin's evening song, the shrieking of the gulls, the heavy thump of Helga's inboard motorboat, the gentle slap-slap of waves against its bow.

"Are you all right?" It was the waitress. She sounded concerned.

"I don't know. I'm not sure…" Her face blurred before me. I caught my breath.

"You want I should call you a cab?"

I nodded.

"You look real bad, honey. If I was you, I'd go right home and go to bed."

"Yes." That sounded like a good idea.

Then somehow a taxi was there and the waitress was helping me in.

"Where to?" asked the driver.

"Tell him where you live, honey."

"At…I have to catch the Union boat…the Union pier, please."

I leaned back then in the seat. I was going home.

I felt drowsy, but just before going to sleep, my whole body jerked, as if suddenly charged by electricity.

I sensed myself shifting into a lower gear. Then I slept.

21

I WAS AWAKENED by someone shaking me gently by the shoulder. I stared into the face of a man I had never seen before.

"You're here. Union pier." I half fell out of the car.

"That's fifty cents." His voice stopped me as I turned to go.

After paying him, I stood blinking in the bright sunshine. Several ships were moored farther down the pier from where I stood at a taxi stand. I recognized the bright orange funnels and black-and-white hulls as being the Union steamship colors. A smell of hot tar mingled with the salt in the air.

I ached. My lower back ached and my legs felt heavy. I had a sense of something about to happen—a teetery feeling.

Without thinking too much about what I was doing, I

went inside the waiting room to buy a ticket. As I stood in line, I thought I saw Nels round the corner of the waiting room, but when I looked again, he was gone.

I gave my ticket to the purser and went up the gangplank of the *Lady Rose*. Standing at the rail, I watched the ropes being cast off. Bells from the wheelhouse signaled the engine room. The engines reversed. As if in a dream, I watched the jade green water stir into white, swirling froth.

The *Lady Rose* was swarming with holiday-makers. Dressed in bright shorts and wearing sunhats, noses covered with white zinc ointment, they ate popcorn and fed the seagulls that followed us out under the Lion's Gate Bridge.

Starting with the upper deck, I covered the entire ship looking for Nels. I peered into groups of people until they stood back in alarm. But I couldn't find him.

My back ached more and more, the pain spreading around to the front and causing me to grunt when it hit. I walked back and forth on the deck. That helped. When I went to the bathroom, an hour's sail out of Vancouver, I saw a trickle of blood behind me in the toilet.

I stared at it, unable to believe what I saw.

It was true. I was bleeding. I found a dime to put in the Kotex machine. Then I went out on deck to look for Nels again.

Nels wasn't on the boat anywhere.

Did he know I was pregnant? Did I tell him? I couldn't remember.

By the time the *Lady Rose* docked at the Landing, I was beyond caring. The cramps were strong and regular. There was a sensation of a string being stretched across inside me, and every cramp pulled it tighter, thinner.

It was going to break soon. And I wanted to be off the boat and alone when it did.

When the *Lady Rose* pulled into the Landing, I could hardly stand up straight. I moved quickly into the crowd of passengers hurrying to get off. I had to take short steps, my knees clenched together. I stayed in the crowd until we were off the pier. Then I headed for the beach trail.

I went up along the bank as far as I could, nearly as far as the meadow where my brothers went to ride Big Red. Leaving the main trail, I followed a path, almost hidden by small alders, right down to the creek.

There was a little clearing near the water, circled with dark, lacy cedars. Birds sang in the forest all around me. A woodpecker hammered directly overhead. There were patches of sunlight and cool shade.

I spent the rest of the afternoon passing clots of blood and resting on the soft mossy ground, and always in the background was the soothing sound of water running over stones. A warm berry smell rose from blackberry vines that ran along moss-covered logs.

Once a brown rabbit popped out of the low bushes, stared for a minute, then hopped away. Small pieces of shredded cone drifted down from a tall fir. Looking up, I saw a squirrel sitting on his haunches, black eyes shining bright.

Then a rapid series of fierce contractions brought me up from lying on my back to a squatting position, and I strained and cried out until I passed—what?

I looked down. And saw there the beginning form of a baby boy.

It lay, a pale bud on the green moss. It was a child with tiny ears, eyes closed with miniature eyelids, a nose, a long back curled on itself, a little boy penis.

I wiped the blood from the tiny body, then splashed water from the creek on it.

And wept.

And bled until I knew I had to stop it somehow. Reaching into the ice-cold water of the creek, I took several stones that had been worn flat and smooth by the running water. Putting my legs up to rest on a log, I laid the cold heavy stones on myself, low, where the cramps were. One more strong contraction, and the afterbirth slipped out. It looked like a pink sponge.

After that the bleeding seemed to stop. I replaced the stones with colder ones from the creek.

I kept the baby near me. He rested like a pale blossom on the emerald moss. I didn't know what I was going to do with him, his body. If I buried him here, he would be dug up by animals. Eaten.

I traced the tiny spine with my finger.

By now the sun was disappearing below the tree tops, and the woods with their sweet berry smell cooled and moistened.

After burying the afterbirth in some soft earth beneath a rotting cedar stump, I wrapped the tiny body in burdock leaves and took it with me.

I found myself following the path down the side of the creek and passing under the bridge that divided Helga's place from ours. Birds were calling out their last songs of the day as my feet kept taking me along, right down to the edge of the ocean.

It was almost sunset, and the beach was deserted. There was Helga's boat tied up to the float. Before I knew it, I had climbed in it, untied the rope and cast off. I rowed out toward Keats Island. When I was halfway there, I pulled the oars and let the boat drift.

The world was golden all around me from the last glow of sunset, and the ocean lay, a sheet of gold, as far as I could see. There wasn't a hint of breeze to mar the surface. It was almost like being in a dream. The hazy blue mountains hung like shrouds over me. Not a sound anywhere.

Rummaging under the stern seat, I found a discarded waxed bread wrapper—perhaps from a lunch Helga had packed for herself—and a broken fishing line, complete with small lead weights. I placed the baby in the wrapper, tied it securely with the fishing line and weights, and let it over the side of the boat.

I let the line slip through my fingers until it reached the water, then sank beneath the surface. The boat rocked with the tiniest of movements.

I watched the package dip, spin for an instant, sink rapidly and disappear down in the deep black water. I let the line go.

Nothing moved on the water. Or below. I sat and watched the sun begin its curve behind the spiky tops of the trees on the headland, saw its red orb halve, quarter, slip over the edge of the world.

I stayed out on the water until night had blotted out everything but the faint outlines of the shore and orange coal oil lights from cottage windows.

Finally I rowed back to the land, the oars cutting flashes of phosphorescence in the night water.

Helga was there on the float when I got back. She helped me tie up the boat, and then she helped me out. I felt weak and dizzy. I tried to speak, to apologize for taking her boat, but all I did was cry.

All the time Helga was saying, "Is okay, is okay," in a soothing voice as we walked up the float, along the beach trail and to her house.

I have a faint recollection of her putting a soft, loose nightgown over my head, of drinking an eggnog, of being tucked into bed. Her eyes were steadfast in the lamplight when she blew it out.

I slept—a deep sleep like a stone being pushed over a cliff, but once the deep stage had passed, I began to dream fitfully. The dreams were images of Nels: Nels laughing, Nels talking...I was trying to reach him, but although I walked and walked, I could never get any closer. He faded back, out of my reach. Then came a kaleidoscope of changing colors: branches, moss, sky, water and a bud-baby that swam before my eyes, glistening with streaks of blood that wouldn't wipe off, seemed even to spread.

I woke crying. The nightgown and the bed were soaked with perspiration. Helga was there in an instant, and she dried me off with a towel, gave me a fresh nightgown, changed the sheets, and poured me a drink of something that tasted of…herbs? I didn't like it.

"No," Helga insisted, refusing to take the glass from my outstretched hand. "Is good for you. Drink."

I drank it down but only to please her. But I found I couldn't go back to sleep. My legs were cramped with pain. What I wanted to do was walk.

We walked, Helga and I, side by side, she with an old jacket over her shoulders and I wearing one of her heavy woolen sweaters. Her hand was ready whenever I stumbled.

The night was cool and dark. Now and then I heard small skitterings in the night stillness—an animal or perhaps a bird. Along the trails, as far as the beach and up the creek, Helga and I walked until I was exhausted and glad to go back, drop into the bed and there, finally, sleep without dreaming.

* * *

In the morning I couldn't seem to waken. I didn't want to. But when Helga said, "Breakfast, come," I had to get up, bleary-eyed and dull, and follow her into the kitchen. She took my breakfast from the warming-shelf above the stove and set the plate before me.

I wasn't hungry. I wasn't anything. I wanted not to bother, or be bothered, or made to care.

Helga sat beside me at the table and buttered my toast. "Eat," she said.

It was only the sight of her hard brown hand lying at rest on the spotless cross-stitch tablecloth and that look of hers that was like love—but simple, without hurt—that made me pick up my knife and fork.

It was grief that was overwhelming me. I hadn't expected it. I thought I would only feel relief.

A boy. Somehow I had thought it would be a girl. All along it seemed—because it was a problem and not wanted—that it had to be a girl.

Helga made me go back to bed for an hour and again, after lunch, another hour's rest. In between resting and eating, I sat outside in the shade of the house. From where I sat, comfortable in a wicker armchair, I could watch Helga weeding in the garden. She used a hoe and worked with a quick chopping motion. She seemed to like padding barefoot in the soft brown soil. Sometimes I could hear her singing to herself in Norwegian.

Hours passed. I slept, I ate, I sat outside in the summer sun. The day ended, passed into another. I lost all sense of time. I only knew that I felt stronger and that Helga was there. She never asked me any questions, and I never told her anything.

Thursday came and with it the realization that I had to get back to work. Helga walked with me to the end of the beach trail to catch the boat, and we stayed there until the very last minute, to avoid being seen by anyone I knew. I was glad to see Mr. Percy go up the wharf before the boat was ready to pull out. When the *Lady Rose* did blow her whistle, I hugged Helga—staying for a moment close to her brown spareness—then ran from the gangplank.

I didn't stay on deck but went below and stayed there until we were well out in the Gap.

22

NELS WAS MARRIED in late July. My mother sent me the newspaper clipping. He married Emma Hoffman, of all people—she of the red hair who works in the telephone office.

"She's years older than Nels," wrote my mother. "I can't imagine what he sees in her. Some people say she's in the family way."

How do I feel? I hurt—a sharp, physical pain just under my ribs. All this time, in the back of my mind, I must have held out some hope that Nels and I would be together again.

Working at the Jolly Jumbo helps the hurt, and so do the people I work with, especially Don. He makes arrangements to have the same days off. We rent bikes and explore

Stanley Park, play pitch-and-putt, go to see Doris Day movies, and sit on benches and watch Kitsilano Showboat.

It is hard to save money, though. Each payday I try to put fifteen dollars in the bank, but more often than not it is only ten. Now at the end of August I have saved only seventy-two dollars, and the tuition fee at nursing school is one hundred and ten dollars. Besides that, students are expected to buy their own books, shoes and stockings, and uniforms. I'm not going to be able to make the September class. I'll have to apply for the January one instead. My marks have come from Victoria in the mail, first classes in everything.

I thought of asking my father for the balance of the tuition fee. He probably would give it to me. But I feel now that I'll never be able to ask him for anything again, although I'm not quite sure why.

I have phoned him once since that time. The clerk at the Campbell River Hotel said he wasn't in. I left a message— "Everything fine. Sheila."—and have tried to put the whole episode out of my mind. It works most of the time if I keep myself busy. And my father doesn't write or phone me, and I am just as happy he doesn't.

Labour Day is our last very busy time at the drive-in. Then I have three days coming to me, and I've decided to go home to visit my mother and brothers. I've written every week. If I'm one day late, my mother phones me from Mr. Percy's store, wondering if I'm all right.

* * *

Mr. Percy has put awnings above the store windows and painted the porch. He has a little more white in his eyebrows, a little rounder paunch under his belt. But his eyes are as bright and astonished looking as ever.

"Well, Sheila," he kept saying every two minutes as we walked up the wharf together the morning I went home. Then he told me all about the happenings in the village. You'd think I'd been away forever.

We stood there in the September sun, and a smell of ripening apples came from the orchard on the other side of the store. Most of its trees are too old to produce anything more than small, hard fruit, but there is one Snow apple tree off by itself that has somehow managed to thrive. Its apples are large, juicy, sweet—much like a McIntosh but larger—and with fine red lines running through a snow-white flesh. I could see the tree from where I stood.

"Are the Snow apples ripe yet?" I asked Mr. Percy.

"Almost. It's funny, Sheila. I've never seen another Snow apple tree on this whole peninsula. Come to think of it, I've never run across it anywhere before. And you've never seen such a crop as it has this year! Can't understand it. Doesn't get any more sun or rain than the other trees."

On my way home I walked through the orchard. Mr. Percy was right about the heavy crop of fruit on the Snow apple tree.

The apples weren't quite ripe. I bit into one. In another couple of weeks they would be sweeter still.

I cut back along the beach. The summer cottages looked forlorn, all closed up for the season. The diving float had been towed away, and I saw it riding behind Shelter Island, where it had been tied up for the winter.

When I got to the bridge between Helga's place and ours, I hung over the rail to watch the migrating salmon crowd up the creek. Some of the fish looked soft already, even though they had not come that far from the salt water.

I was afraid to go home. Would my mother be able to tell by looking at me what had happened since I last saw her? Or was it possible that she could understand? If what my father said was true, that they hadn't married…

Pep came bounding up the trail to meet me, racing round and round in circles and barking until my mother came out the back door to see what was the matter. She shaded her eyes against the sun.

"Is that you, Sheila?" She made it sound as if I'd been away for a year and never sent a word home. It was hard not to cry. I bent down to scratch Pep behind the ears.

Straightening up, I said, "Just home for a few days, Mom. Saved up my time off."

Nothing had changed, it seemed. The door was left open to catch the thin yellow September sunlight, and it lit the varnished plywood walls, showing clearly the swirls in the wood. There was a bowl of tawny chrysanthemums on the kitchen table. Their sharp dry aroma was like smoke. A golden bantam hen stood on the doorsill and put her head on one side, watching us with yellow eyes.

My mother was in the middle of canning pears. I took up a paring knife to help her, and we worked together, the smooth peelings falling from our knives like butter.

"What about nursing school, Sheila?" she asked. "Have you got your application in?"

"Yes," I said, "but I won't be able to get in until January's class. I haven't been able to save enough money. I thought I could but…"

"How much money do you need?"

I explained.

"That's not much," she said. "Maybe something will turn up."

As I sat across the kitchen table from my mother, peeling pears, their smell in the air between us, I became aware that there was an aloneness now dividing my mother and me.

I no longer believe what she told me about life, about being a woman. I see now that much of her thinking is colored by her upbringing and by her frustrations and disappointments with my father. And that because she thinks I am like him, she tried to get back at him through me.

But I am neither one of them—not my mother, not my father.

The boys came in from school. I could hardly believe that Tom had grown so tall in just two months. His voice had deepened, and he had an Adam's apple I'd never noticed before.

"You must have grown six inches!" I told him. "What was it? The hard work in the mines at Trail?"

He told me about school.

"I've decided to go on to university. I'd like to go into engineering. Working at Trail this summer convinced me of that. And I made fantastic money there!" His voice was steady. It no longer broke unexpectedly at the end of a sentence.

"You all set to go into nursing school?" he asked. Then when I told him about it, he said, "I don't know. It doesn't seem right. Here it is September, and for the first time you're not going back to school."

As soon as I decently could, I went over to see Helga. She was preparing several large salmon for smoking. Hurrying over to me at once, skinny scratched legs showing beneath a gunny sack apron, her brown face broke into a smile.

I put my arms around her and cried, and so did she. It sounded rusty, as if she hadn't cried for years and years.

Then we walked to the house where she made a pot of coffee, and while we were waiting for it, she brought out a tissue-wrapped parcel. It held a white cardigan sweater.

"For when you are being a nurse," she told me, holding it up against me to measure the length. It is a beautiful sweater, of the finest white wool and every stitch perfect.

"Oh, Helga," I said, "thank you! It's the most beautiful sweater I've ever seen."

"Yah," she said matter-of-factly. "Is good. I make pattern from my own head. How long you stay?"

"Three days."

"Will be finished. Yah, you take it back when you go."

* * *

I hadn't been back in Vancouver for more than a week when Mrs. Williams came rapping at my door early one morning.

"Uhhh?" I managed through the fog of waking up.

"Your mother's here," she said. "I'm giving her a cup of tea in the kitchen. Come on, love, wake up!"

My mother! I looked around my room with a groan. It was a mess. Clothes everywhere. I kicked some shoes under the bed and hastily straightened the covers and bedspread.

My mother and Mrs. Williams were having a good chat. You'd think they had known each other for years. I filled a bowl with cornflakes, found an orange and sat down with them. But I was still blurred with sleep and had trouble following their conversation. It lapped around me like water.

"So what do you think of that, Sheila?" Mrs. Williams' voice brought me back.

"Sorry—"

"Your mother selling her piano so that you'll have the money for the tuition fee to nursing school."

Both my mother and Mrs. Williams were smiling happily. They looked at me, waiting for my response.

"I wish…I wish you hadn't done that," I said, trying to sound more gracious than I felt.

"It's done," my mother answered. "I thought you'd be happy about this. She's like her father that way," she explained to Mrs. Williams. "I did and did for that man and never a word of gratitude."

"It's not that, Mom! It's that the piano means so much to you!"

It was more than that. Having successfully interfered between Nels and me, how dared she interfere again in my life! Did she think that this would make up for what had happened?

"Besides, it's too late to get into the September class now. It starts in a week. Registration's closed. They'll be filled up."

"People drop out at the last minute. Why don't you phone them and find out?"

I thought I might as well go through the motions to please her. I dialed the nursing school, asked for the Director of Nursing, and explained the situation.

"You are in luck!" The voice was clear, professional. It came over the receiver loud enough for both my mother and Mrs. Williams to hear. They sat up, alert, and looked pleased with themselves.

"I've just this minute put down the phone," went on the Director of Nursing, "and one of the applicants has decided to go on to university instead. Now just let me check your application in the January file. Oh, yes, here it is.

Sheila Brary. Yes, well, your marks are excellent. No problem there. Do you think you could get three letters of recommendation by Friday..."

My mother left soon afterwards.

"I have some shopping to do before I catch the evening boat home," she explained. Then she counted out the hundred and ten dollars for the tuition. It was all in small bills, and she smoothed each one out carefully.

After she'd gone and Mrs. Williams and I were washing up the few dishes, Mrs. Williams turned to me.

"She's a wonderful mother to have made that sacrifice for you."

* * *

Before going in training, I made one more trip to the Landing to get the three letters of recommendation.

Now, in the middle of September, the Snow apples were ripe—huge, juicy, delicious. Red on the outside; inside their whiteness was veined with red. As I bit into one, the sharp, sweet, tangy taste seemed to me to capture the essence of the Landing—unique and beautiful.

One letter of recommendation was given to me by the school principal. The second one I got from the priest who has been newly appointed to the peninsula and who gave it to me not because he knows I have a good character but because he knows my mother has, and the third one was from Dr. Howard.

My mother seemed glad to see me. I found out that part

of her good spirits was due to news she had. William Mann, her correspondence course instructor in Victoria, had sent her the addresses of two or three poetry magazines and had suggested she send some of her own poems to them.

She had sold two of them to *Fiddlehead*.

"I didn't know you write poetry, Mom!"

"I used to. Before I met your father. Anyway, it was one of the assignments in the correspondence course."

"They must be good to be published."

"I have an idea for a children's story that I want to try out. Mr. Mann said he would check it over for me when I finished, if I wanted him to."

She looked happier and more alive than I'd ever seen her.

When I left on the boat for Vancouver, Tom saw me off. It's something he never did ordinarily.

"Just imagine, Tom. I'm going back to school after all. Though I still wish Mom hadn't sold the piano to pay my tuition." The boat sounded its warning whistle.

Tom looked hard at me.

"Is that why you haven't said anything to me? Not even thanks?"

"What are you talking about?"

Tom was slow to answer.

"I gave Mom the money to give to you. She sold the piano afterwards. It had nothing to do with you. She must have told you!"